HOTEL FOR MURDER

The coroner and the sheriff came out of the office. Standing with the deputy, they watched the attendants exit with the body. Hat in hand, Sheriff Virgil Tarrant spoke softly. "I'll be leaving with the coroner, but my deputy will stick around to take your statements. For now, all of you stay in the hotel."

"Sheriff." I raised my hand, feeling like a student. "I have a magic act to get to in Allentown."

Sheriff Tarrant sized me up like a boxer checking out an untested opponent. He smiled, and I knew he'd decided it was heavyweight versus flyweight. "If you try to leave, I'll put a slug in you before you reach the door. You'll be deader than that Bozo in the safe."

Other Avon Books by
Patrick A. Kelley

SLEIGHTLY MURDER

SLEIGHTLY LETHAL

PATRICK A. KELLEY

AVON
PUBLISHERS OF BARD, CAMELOT, DISCUS AND FLARE BOOKS

SLEIGHTLY LETHAL is an original publication of Avon Books. This work has never before appeared in book form. This work is a novel. Any similarity to actual persons or events is purely coincidental except for the universally recognized magicians and sleight-of-hand artists who are mentioned in passing.

AVON BOOKS
A division of
The Hearst Corporation
1790 Broadway
New York, New York 10019

Copyright © 1986 by Patrick A. Kelley
Published by arrangement with the author
Library of Congress Catalog Card Number: 85-91508
ISBN: 0-380-89727-X

First Avon Printing, June 1986

AVON TRADEMARK REG. U. S. PAT. OFF. AND IN OTHER COUNTRIES,
MARCA REGISTRADA, HECHO EN U. S. A.

Printed in the U.S.A.

K-R 10 9 8 7 6 5 4 3 2 1

To Tom Ogden,
whose magic is humorous and whose humor is magical.

Special thanks to Bill Eldred for steering me clear of the Land of the Lost Chapters.

And thanks again to my wife, Marilyn, for total honesty when I sorely needed it.

CHAPTER ONE

A gutted office building and the hotel were all that was left of the block. Because its neighbors had been razed, the Fitch Hotel, with its cold gray stone and dirty windows, now looked forbidding, like a tomb. I just hoped to hell there wasn't a body inside.

The two-hour drive had exhausted me. The van had threatened to shake apart every time I exceeded seventy, but I'd kept it floored. Although the radio had been dead a year, I had periodically pounded the dash, hoping to revive it long enough for a newscast. No luck.

At every public telephone sign, I had pulled over, but the Fitch's number was always busy. Using the same quarter each time, I began to think of it as an old friend that would stick with me forever.

Without the phone stops, I could have arrived half an hour sooner. But I was obsessed with this question: was Quimp the Clown dead . . . murdered?

The right front tire rolled up on the curbing, and the van lurched to a stop. Glass shattered behind me, followed by a dripping sound. A whiskey smell filled the van. Another magic trick ruined. This time my favorite: Think-A-Drink. I'd clean it up later.

I trotted under the stained awning of the Fitch, noting that the knee-high lion sculpture—the one that had greeted magicians from around the world with its stony roar—looked as though someone had savaged it with a ball-peen hammer.

A sign, stapled to a stick, leaned against the lion. "Save the Fitch," it demanded. The sign's owner must have been out to lunch. The doorman was gone, too.

Inside, the lobby was as hushed as a warehouse. I made my way to the front desk through a narrow passage created by stacked crates, cardboard boxes, and furniture. The carpeting was ripped in several places, and the walls had deep gashes. A sign on the elevator told me not to use it. The place smelled musty, like a basement. If the upper floors were anything like the lobby, the Fitch's three-star rating was a goner. It was hard to believe that, on my last visit, this room teemed with guests, mostly magicians clamoring to show off their latest.

At the desk I was greeted by a pair of propped-up feet and a face covered with newspaper. Soft snoring came from under the newsprint. At least this body was alive. Lights blinked on the switchboard behind the desk. Why let phone calls interrupt a good snooze? Three college textbooks lay unopened at the end of the counter.

The snorer's paper was three days old, as were the ones on sale in the rack beside the desk. I speculated on the standard price for three-day-old papers. Less than day-old bread?

The counter had no bell, so I cleared my throat. When the snoring got louder, I snatched away the paper.

The clerk's feet slipped off the counter, smacking the floor. She looked to be twenty and was pretty . . . and pretty ticked-off at being disturbed.

Around her neck was a short gray scarf that looked like a cowboy's bandanna with fringe. She wore putty-colored jeans that stopped at mid-calf, revealing browned skin, a July suntan in April. Carefully folding her newspaper, she pretended not to have been asleep. I hoped she wasn't majoring in theatre. Her acting was lousy.

"Is Jack in?"

"Mr. O'Connell's out to lunch." She was still sleepy-voiced.

"With the picketer?"

Her stare was blank.

"Never mind. Why is Jack *out* to lunch when he's got—" For the first time I noticed that the hotel restaurant was dark. No fried smell or clink of dishes.

"The whole place is closed?" I asked.

"Yes. And no. We still have some guests, but we aren't accepting new ones. If you want, I'll arrange reservations at another hotel."

"I don't want a room. I'm looking for—" There was no elegant way to say *dead clown*. "—a friend. There are people staying here?"

"Yes, personal guests of Mr. O'Connell. If you ask me, he's gone to a lot of bother for nothing."

"Is Quimp still around?"

She thawed at the mention of a familiar name. "Yes. He's why the hotel isn't totally shut down yet."

"Is he all right?"

"He's fine. He's in back, but can't be disturbed."

Jack's office was behind her. The rear of his office opened onto a conference room where Jack used to conduct staff meetings. Now his entire staff seemed to consist of one coed in knickers. My curiosity about the hotel's fate edged out my concern for the clown.

"Was there a Magicade this year?"

"Yes, the convention ended three days ago. Mr. O'Connell called it his last hoorah. He let all the employees go, thinking he wouldn't need them. When these guests decided to stay extra days, he hired me, through an employment agency. This is only my second day."

She told me she was Allison King, a community college student, major undecided. Endeavoring to explain away her nap, she said she currently held down three part-time jobs.

"The Fitch will be demolished, like the rest of the block?" I asked.

"Yep."

I asked if any magicians had rallied to save the hotel. She said she didn't know why they would. Apparently the Fitch's show-biz tradition was not nearly so important to

Allison as checking herself in her compact mirror. She patted dark curls into place, but decided against a facial touch-up. Only several hours of staying awake would erase the puffiness.

She clicked shut her compact and said, "So you're worried about Quimp? I bet you saw *Magazine Tonite.* "

I nodded.

"We got swamped after that TV show. I had to pull the switchboard plugs. Mailgrams and telegrams poured in, all asking about Quimp. He didn't think people would misunderstand him, and he regrets saying it now. You see, he was speaking of death only in a figurative sense."

No, I didn't see. But I accepted it as yet another example of Quimp's eccentricity. I breathed easier, now that the only death to contend with was the Fitch's. I'd miss the hotel, but not like I would Quimp.

Quimp—the genius.

Quimp—the entertainment institution.

Quimp—one of the world's greatest clowns.

"How about a favor?" I asked. "My name is Harry Colderwood. Could you check if any packages arrived for me?"

She didn't recognize my name. I felt odd.

My props were breaking faster than I could replace them. Most were specially made, and I had to order them months in advance. Because I constantly traveled, the Magic Castle in L.A. and the Mostly Magic nightclub in New York City generously held packages for me. The Fitch did the same. Although it had been five years since I last attended a Magicade, I managed to visit the Fitch a couple of times a year.

"I'll check, Mr. Collingwood."

"Colderwood," I corrected.

After she stepped into the office, I opened the hefty guest book. In addition to Quimp's name (scrawled in three-inch red letters), there were a half-dozen magicians I hadn't seen in years. One name stopped me cold: Cate Elliott Fleming.

"Cate?" I said aloud. "At the Magicade?"

Allison returned with a slip of paper. "No packages, but here's a note with your name on it."

The memo, in Jack's jagged handwriting, explained that a Mr. Jeffers had phoned for me and would try again later.

Jeffers, you won't find me.

My vow lacked heart.

"Allison, if Jeffers calls back, don't tell him I was here. Got that?"

"Sure."

"Did you check the safe for packages?"

"It was locked."

"Good sign. Jack locks it only when it contains valuables."

I looked at my watch, deciding Allentown couldn't wait much longer.

"Jack wouldn't have given you the combination, because you're new here. He once told me that because he was always forgetting it, he kept it written on a card in his middle desk drawer beneath the plastic organizer tray. How about looking? Then you can go back to sleep."

"I doubt that. I'm wide-awake, thanks to you."

With no qualms about going through her employer's desk, she returned to the office.

I heard a drawer open; then, "Found it."

"Need help?"

"No. I'll manage."

I looked at Jack's memo. Its letterhead was a fine-lined drawing of the Fitch, accurate down to the detail of the sculpted lion. No picket sign, though. No rusted-out van parked curbside, either.

I again looked at Cate Fleming's delicate signature in the book.

Cate Fleming *and* Jeffers. In the same day. Small world. And it was now threatening to suffocate me.

I heard a clunk of the safe's handle. The combination had posed no problem for Allison.

Its contents did.

Her scream was a siren, starting low, then rising in pitch and intensity.

I vaulted over the counter, tangling my legs in Allison's chair. It scored a two-point takedown on me, and I rolled, hitting the floor with my back. I flung the chair off my chest.

Entering the office, I saw the black safe in the far corner. Allison stood with her back to it, arms in a tight X across her chest. She slowly twisted from side to side, in denial of what was behind her. Of what was in the safe.

His eyes were closed, and he was crammed into the safe so tightly that knees touched chin. The trademarks were unmistakable: threadbare hat, glistening red sphere nose, dotted necktie above tattered collar—and the name tag on his vest: "Quimp."

I shuttled Allison out the door and shut it, muffling her crying.

Did Roselle have a 911 system? Did the town even have a police force? The phone wouldn't respond when I dialed "0." I remembered about the switchboard.

Back out at the registration desk, I inserted switchboard plugs until most of the lights stopped flashing. I righted the toppled chair, but Allison wouldn't sit down, wouldn't stop sobbing.

Returning to the office, I dialed again. This time an operator answered.

I avoided looking at the iron coffin.

Poor Quimp. His prediction *had* come true.

Poor Allison. Her prediction, too, had come true. She'd sleep no more today.

CHAPTER TWO

My breakfast earlier that morning had consisted of black coffee and a newspaper. After that I got my income tax prepared, watched a VCR demonstration, and learned that Quimp the Clown feared being murdered—all without leaving the Lewis Brothers Department Store in Frederick, Maryland. Ah, the convenience of one-stop shopping.

My hooded sweatshirt and worn work boots must have confused the tax man, but he got down to business once he recognized me. It happens less and less nowadays.

He told me he used to watch me on television, but couldn't remember how many years ago. He said his favorite routine was the one where I secretly handcuffed audience volunteers to chairs and each other while simultaneously picking their pockets. He asked why I was getting my taxes done at a department store.

"I travel so much, it's tough to rely on one regular accountant. Your corporation has offices all over the country, you're schooled in the latest tax laws, and you're quick. No appointments, just walk in. Plus you're cheap. Cheap is important right now."

My candor embarrassed him, and he shifted in his chair. At moments like this it galled me to think of the tape of my never-aired TV special rotting away in a network storage room.

"Mr. Colderwood, cigarettes are not a legal deduction. I'll cross them out."

"Let them be. They're part of my act. Watch."

I plucked a lit cigarette from the air.

"Damn," I said. "Lucky Strike. I was trying for a Camel. If you think quitting smoking is hard, consider the magician's dilemma. My next cigarette is always hanging in thin air. I don't even need a lighter." I took a hardy puff.

"Okay, we'll declare them a prop expense. Wow, you sure go through a lot."

"I do lots of shows. Check how many one-night stands I played last year."

"Hmmm. You see quite a bit of the country."

"More than I care to."

His nameplate identified him as "Mr. Templin." He wore a blue suit with pin stripes as hard to see as the fine print on my last manager's contract. His glasses were sensible tortoiseshells, and his hair was a neat cluster of poodle curls. His only unkempt feature was a hedge mustache.

"I assume 'Jack Daniel's' is the product, not a person?"

"Correct."

He tapped his pen on his lips.

"What's wrong? I use it in my act. Except for kiddy shows."

"I'm questioning the *amount* of the deduction."

"Ever hear of Think-A-Drink Hoffman? Name any drink—soft or alcoholic—and he'd pour you a glass. Over and over. All from one pitcher of water."

"But the only drink you list is Jack Daniel's."

"It's a new trick for me. Jack Daniel's is all I know so far. Test me. Think of any drink . . . as long as it's you-know-what."

He rose from his chair, patting the air with his hands. "Please, it'll hurt my credibility if my cubicle smells like you-know-what."

He continued scanning my list. "You use livestock."

"No."

"But you list doves."

"I've dropped all animals. Too hard to care for. I learned the hard way. One night I got to practicing Think-A-Drink and forgot to take my doves out of the van . . . for two days. I woke up on my motel floor at two in the afternoon. That was in Phoenix, and the temperature hit a hundred-five. Besides the doves, I also forgot about a show booked a hundred miles down the road.''

"The doves?''

I took off an imaginary hat and placed it over my heart. "The whole dozen.''

"Says *two* dozen here.''

"I practiced Think-A-Drink a lot last year.''

Other last-minute filers sat waiting outside his cubicle, but Templin was in no rush. My case intrigued him.

"If you're audited, I advise you—''

"*When* I'm audited. It happens yearly, like clockwork.''

"Then I needn't caution you about playing games with the IRS. Listing Jack Daniel's and dead doves will draw considerable attention.''

"I always play games with the IRS.''

"It's your funeral. I'm here to compute, not judge.''

He read further in my ledger, humming softly. His improvised tune shot off-key when he reached the column listing my income. He took off his glasses and spoke in a low voice. "I shouldn't say this, but you must be crack-brained, Mr. Colderwood. Your income is mostly *cash.*'' He spoke in the tone of a preacher admonishing an unrepentant sinner.

"So? That's how I'll pay you, too. Cash.'' I reached in the air and produced another smoking Lucky. "Whoops. Wrong hand.'' In the other a crisp ten-spot materialized.

"What I'm saying, man, is that cash is virtually untraceable. You could declare just a fraction of it.''

"Uh-uh. That final figure *is* what I earned—the unpainted truth. I *never* play games with the IRS.''

"But you just said . . .'' He gave up trying to understand and again immersed himself in my figures. His finger stopped on one entry. "This fee from Mrs. Wanda Morrow is considerably bigger than the others. Was it a magic show?''

"No. I performed a personal service. I found out who killed her husband."

"Oh," Templin said, trying to sound matter-of-fact. "Were there other personal services last year?"

"A few."

"We could list them as a separate business."

"No. It was using my magician's skill, just in a different manner."

"Mrs. Morrow paid well. You should do more work like this."

"No. Check the expense column. You'll see I lost money on that job. I lost even more in non-monetary ways."

He shrugged, replaced his glasses, and jabbed at his calculator keyboard. Then he rechecked his work. The results disturbed him.

The paltry bottom line was stark evidence that my full-evening theatre shows were history. Templin now knew why I dressed this way: I was my own roadie, loading and unloading props myself. No more assistants and stage crews.

Signing my return, he said, "When's your next TV shot?"

"Fifteen seconds before I mail this."

He quoted his fee, and I made good my promise by plucking the exact amount out of the air, burning myself on a stray Lucky that insisted on appearing. I threw in a liberal tip, extracted this time from my wallet. Anemic, the wallet slid too easily into my hip pocket. Besides too little cash, it was thin because there were empty spaces where I used to keep credit cards until I lost them. There were also spaces for friends' pictures, until I lost them too—the friends, that is, not the pictures. I wished the money-plucking trick were real.

"Are you working locally?" he asked.

I had never gone so long between big paying dates. My last job had been in an all-star vaudeville revival. I had never heard of the other "all-stars." They were too young to remember when TV was all black-and-white, let alone when vaudeville thrived.

More and more now, I whimsically considered performing on street corners and passing the hat. Only I didn't own a hat.

"I'm headed for Allentown. I've got a new manager who's breaking me into trade shows."

"Conventions and expositions?"

"That's right."

"Some advice: three-piece suits aren't costumes, so don't try deducting them next year."

"I don't own any yet."

Then, in the tax preparer's cubicle beside the credit office of Lewis Brothers Department Store, I heard Quimp's voice. It was only for five seconds, but it was undeniably him. I hastily thanked Templin and rushed into the shopping area to search for the speaker that had blared that voice.

Quimp. It had been years since I last heard him. The public *never* had that privilege. With pantomime as his language, he never broke silence while performing.

I walked down an aisle cluttered with bikes and barbells, listening for his voice. All I heard was the PA's hoarse plea for Mrs. Phipps to report to carpeting. I followed the arrows to Home Entertainment.

All but one of the two dozen televisions were tuned to Phil Donahue. From TV to TV, Phil's hair ranged from sparkling silver to rest-home gray. One dissenting set displayed a frozen close-up of Quimp.

"Help you?" The salesman wore marshmallow-white shoes and a tie so thick it looked upholstered.

"This clown's on tape?"

"Yes."

"Could you rewind it?"

"His makeup looks great, doesn't it? I saved the cassette to show off this model's exceptional color. Fair warning— our sale ends today." He hit Rewind and launched his pitch before I could object.

When Quimp came alive on-screen, I tuned out the salesman's drone. Les Cook, the emcee for the syndicated *Magazine Tonite,* was interviewing Quimp in front of the Fitch Hotel in Roselle, Maryland. The broadcast was three days old.

Quimp's speaking jarred me. It was as if a character in a silent film had suddenly burst into song. He expressed delight at being honored once again at the Magicade Convention. He answered questions about what clowning meant to him and how newcomers could become clowns.

When queried about his future, Quimp grew solemn, placing a gloved hand to his temple. "I don't believe in psychics or fortune-tellers."

Amen.

"But I'll make a prediction," he said. "Quimp is not long for this world. Somebody plans to do away with him. I won't check out of this hotel alive."

Suddenly he snapped back into his silly character, flashing his patented smile, the one that seemed to swallow half his face. He drenched the shocked Les Cook with seltzer water. The crew snickered in the background, and the cameraman was laughing so hard he couldn't hold his Steadicam steady.

When the salesman pushed the pause button, again freezing the Quimp image, I fled, casing the store for the nearest exit. The salesman dogged behind, singing praises of redder reds, greener greens, and easier credit.

Beneath Quimp's frivolity, I had sensed futility. He was serious about not leaving that hotel alive. I dialed the Fitch's number from a mall pay phone. Busy.

A seventy-mile drive lay ahead. The murderer had a three-day jump on me, and Quimp needed more protection than a seltzer bottle. A hell of a lot more.

CHAPTER THREE

For the second time that day I gazed at the frozen face of Quimp the Clown. This time, however, he was framed not by a TV screen, but by the black edges of the floor safe. Outside the office, Allison's screams had waned to jerky sobs.

The operator gave me the sheriff's number, and I dialed it. Busy. I disconnected and tried again. It rang, but no answer. With the phone pressed to my ear, I walked to the safe. Ignoring the quiver in my hand, I pressed Quimp's neck. No pulse. Makeup came off on my fingers. I shivered and wiped it on my trousers.

Jack's office was cramped. A worn path in the carpet led from the entrance over to the desk, then to the conference-room door. A bare coatrack stood on one side of the desk, an empty trash can on the other. Behind the desk a metal bookshelf displayed canted rows of books, mostly almanacs dating from as far back as 1961. Jack probably bought the desk and the shelf from the same discount house. The desktop was a halfhearted wood imitation, with nothing on it but the phone, a dirty coffee cup, and an ashtray loaded with cigar stubs. On the floor in front of the safe was the creased file card containing the combination.

As the phone rang on, I thought about Quimp's age. The makeup had always hidden his years, but surely he was no more than forty-five. How many audiences, from preschool tots to sophisticated nightclub patrons, would now be deprived of his madcap gags? How many more—

The conference-room doorknob rotated with a rattle. I dropped the phone, and by the time the latch clicked, I was flat on the floor behind the desk.

"Hello," the phone on the desk said. The sheriff's office had finally answered.

The door brushed along the carpet, and more than one person walked into the office, making hollow clomps that sounded like wooden shoes. A Dutch hit squad?

The last person to enter didn't clomp, but walked with light, confident steps.

"I guess everything's all right. I still think you should have waited in there." The man's voice was husky, filled with weariness, not fear. After a long silence, he said, "Oh, Jesus! Who's that? Stay back. Get back in there. You too, Marcus."

Marcus?

I stood up and saw there were five of them.

They stared at me with incredulity.

I stared back with more incredulity.

We had a regular goddam incredulity duel.

They were quadruplets-plus-one. Four were dressed and made up like the dead man in the safe—four Quimps with four ragged hats, four shredded neckties, four pairs of size eighteen maroon-and-white saddle oxfords, and four Quimp name tags.

One clown was armed with a five-foot foam rubber hammer. I believed he'd use it if provoked—the perfect defense against giant Styrofoam nails.

Who was the clown in the safe? Not Quimp, I thought.

None of the other clowns was Quimp either.

The fifth person, the one without makeup, was the real Quimp. Dressed in a V-neck cashmere and baggy corduroys, he looked more like a history teacher than a renowned entertainer.

He stared at the safe, then wordlessly asked me for an explanation. When I shrugged, he said, "Harry. It's . . . it's good to see you." This pantomime king was never great with words.

"We got a lot to talk about, Marcus." I always called him by his real name when he was out of costume.

I picked up the phone.

"What the hell is going on there?" the voice said, impatiently pinching each word.

"There's been a death at the Fitch Hotel. Possible homicide."

With sadness, I thought of my favorite childhood toy. I had played with it daily until it finally broke. The circus music would still play when I cranked it, but the lid no longer sprang open. I was heartbroken.

I really loved that jack-in-the-box. I mourned the day the little clown inside died.

CHAPTER FOUR

Through the lobby door I could see my van, one wheel still atop the curb. Jack O'Connell, the hotel owner, was sitting across from me. A pudgy man in his early sixties, he wore a short-sleeve white shirt that hung loosely, like a sheet. His hair was the same color as his shirt. Give him a beard and red suit, and he could have made a fortune delivering gifts in December.

Actually, many magicians *did* think of him as Santa. The perfect audience, he always clapped and laughed until his eyes turned to slits. Now his eyes were wide and sober.

His cigar looked expensive but smelled cheap. In self-defense, I slid a cigarette out of my pack and lit it. No magic today.

I had already given a statement to Sheriff Virgil Tarrant and his deputy. At the other end of the lobby, by the restaurant entrance, the four clowns crowded around one mirror, removing makeup. I hadn't recognized any of them yet. Just as well. I was in no mood for a reunion.

Marcus Spillman stood with them, arms crossed, looking at Jack and me. We avoided his gaze.

While I was on the phone to the sheriff's, the clown with the jumbo hammer had taken charge, herding Spillman and the others back into the conference room, closing the door. Then, hammer held high, he stood silent guard over me, as though I were a dangerous animal. The sheriff and his deputy arrived at the hotel within fifteen minutes.

The coroner showed up ten minutes later and installed

himself in the office with the sheriff, his deputy, and the body. When Jack returned from lunch, he was met by a lobby full of clowns, a hysterical Allison, and two men wearing stars. After filling him in on the discovery in the safe, the sheriff took Jack aside and questioned him.

After the officers calmed Allison and took her statement, she fled with her schoolbooks, informing Jack on the way out that she was quitting.

"Any idea who the dead man is?" I finally asked Jack. We had made only small talk thus far.

"None. Spillman and the four clowns are the only ones that stayed on after the convention."

"Are you sure they're the same four? Their makeup's still on."

"We'll wait and see." He drew on his cigar, lapsing into sullenness.

Jack O'Connell was a magic-lover who never did magic himself. He had turned the Fitch into a gathering place for magicians, even though it was miles from a major city. Nonstop magic surrounded guests at the Fitch from check-in to check-out. The lobby, restaurant, and bar always overflowed with wonderworkers pulling bouquets from nowhere, finding chosen cards, and burning and restoring borrowed handkerchiefs.

Though far from the hotel's only income, magic gave the Fitch its ambiance. Like a jazz club, on any night you never knew who'd be sitting in at the bar, giving a free show.

The hotel annually hosted the Magicade Convention. Over twenty years ago, an unnamed magician (some credit Harry Blackstone, Sr.) said to Jack, "This place is like a perpetual magic convention. Why not actually hold one here?"

Jack supposedly said, "How do you put a thousand magicians in eighty rooms?"

Three drinks later, Jack answered his own question. "It could be a small, closed affair. If you want to come, you gotta earn it."

Only fifty magicians and variety entertainers (jugglers, clowns, ventriloquists, and so on) received invitations each year to the Magicade. A panel of magic buffs selected the guest list. Fame and prowess were important considerations, but a unique contribution to magic was also a crucial factor.

Jack said to hell with those who cried elitism. Only a few did. Entertainers coveted a Magicade invitation, and it became the magic world's equivalent of an Oscar nomination.

To be a paid performer at the Magicade was a supreme honor. I had often attended the convention, but was a hired act only once, five years ago. That was the same year the network pulled my TV special from their schedule. Win some. Lose some.

Quimp, who used simple but superbly performed prestidigitation in his act, held the record for the most consecutive Magicade engagements.

Jack's cigar was now half its original length, and he seemed intent on turning it to ash in record time. I felt like an intruder for speaking. "The Magicade was a smash again this year?"

"Yes. As expected, Quimp shined. Up until he made that . . . that announcement. I still say our best year was when Milbourne Christopher, Doug Henning, and you performed. Couldn't make it again this year, eh?"

"No."

He concentrated on replenishing the smoky fog surrounding him. Then he said, "Where were you the last *four* years? You're not supposed to disappear after you make guest of honor."

"Commitments, Jack. Haven't you been following my career? I've made the papers a few times."

"I usually read just the sports and the front page. Skip the entertainment section altogether."

"The graph of my career shows a steady downhill trend. If that graph were a cardiogram, I'd have been legally dead two years ago."

"I didn't say I *haven't* read about you. Just not in the entertainment section."

"Forget about those incidents. They have nothing to do with my career."

"So? Start a new one."

"No way," I said, too emphatically.

"Ha! A new career." He enjoyed those words. I hated them. "All your Magicade invitations come back stamped Address Unknown. Even after you'd update us with new addresses, they'd still come back. How long can you keep up this pace?"

"Forever. I'm magic. Right?"

For the first time I noticed our voices echoing. Echoes didn't belong in the Fitch. I rubbed my finger along the chair's vinyl, leaving a clean trail in the dust.

"I see you've taken your own advice, Jack. Your pace has definitely changed. You're really closing the Fitch?"

"Not voluntarily."

"Then why?"

"They've pulled the magic carpet out from under us, Harry. The municipal council condemned the whole block. No exceptions."

"I saw that abandoned picket sign outside."

"The guy who carried that was from the county historical society. He walked back and forth for a few weeks, but I haven't seen him for two days. Despair got the best of him. They've ripped down everything but the hotel and the Edison Office Building. They're still bickering about what to build on this site. A parking lot, maybe a playground. Hell, the Fitch *was* a playground. For magicians, anyway."

"You won't relocate?"

He laughed at my question. "If I were your age, maybe. I'm just glad they held off long enough so we could hold this last Magicade. When Marcus made his stupid announcement, I decided to stay open a few days longer."

Sam Wirfel, the deputy, emerged from the office. The lobby quieted, and heads turned as he circled stiffly to the front of the registration desk. He wore dull, metal-framed glasses that kept sliding down. His uniform, with its proud insignias and shiny buttons, made him look like a bellman.

"I bet he was told to keep an eye on us," Jack said, cigar clinched in teeth.

Wirfel, in his late twenties, was about five years younger than me. He looked as if he knew the law—verse and chapter—but nothing about the practicalities of enforcing it.

"The coroner and Sheriff Tarrant will be done soon," Wirfel said.

"Want to make a break for it, Jack?" I whispered. "His glasses are thick, and he's probably a lousy shot." The deputy cocked his head, trying to overhear.

Jack nodded, but, being a solid citizen, decided not to bolt. Instead, he put both feet up on the round Formica table in front of him.

One clown, out of makeup, struck up a conversation with Spillman. A nervous chipmunk of a man, he repeatedly clutched Spillman's arm as they talked. I recognized him as Gregory Hodge, a collector of magic memorabilia and apparatus. He was no performer, and thoroughly butchered the only trick I ever saw him do. Never before had I seen him without a coat and tie. Usually immaculately groomed, his hair rose in jagged clumps from hours of wearing the clown hat. Traces of makeup still spotted his neck.

Spillman excused himself and, hands in pockets, came over to us, nodding to the deputy in passing. Short, and built like a gymnast, Spillman moved with athletic fluidity. At one time he featured acrobatics in his act.

"This the smoking section?" he said, fanning his hand through Jack's curtain of smoke. He sat down beside me.

"Hello, Marcus. Jack still hasn't told me why you and your band of imitators are here."

"I'd like to know why you're here, too. You're the last person I expected to find in that office. No, wrong. The last person I expected is still there. In the safe, to be precise."

"I rushed over from Frederick because you said on *Magazine Tonite* you were going to be murdered. For a minute I believed it. Who is that dead man, Marcus? Jack doesn't know."

"I don't either." He pointed at the four clowns across the lobby. "All present and accounted for. We clowns, Jack, Allison, and now you, were the only ones in the hotel today."

His eyebrows compressed into inverted V's. With makeup for exaggeration, he could easily have conveyed that same bewildered expression to an audience of thousands.

"Marcus, before I commit you to the Yo-Yo Factory, tell me why you said you were going to be murdered."

Yo-Yo Factory, the title of a Quimp sketch, meant sanitarium.

"I raised hell after that broadcast. They cut the part of the interview where I explained myself. I never said murder. Rather, I said that someone was going to do away with *Quimp*. I wasn't talking about Marcus Spillman. I'm *Spillman*, not Quimp. Quimp is a role I play, and I've played it much too long. What good actor plays just one role? Quimp bores me, so I'm giving him up. In fact, I'm giving him away. I'm sick of people getting the two of us confused. So I'm giving up clowning. I'm doing away with Quimp."

Despite what he thought, I never got his two sides confused. I loved Quimp and could endlessly watch his antics, but I found Marcus Spillman tediously aloof. If he really had been murdered, I would have mourned much more for Quimp than for Marcus Spillman.

Jack said, "He's not *giving* Quimp away, he's selling him like a used car. He dropped that bombshell at the end of his Fire Hydrant sketch. He just walked to the edge of the platform in the bar, grabbed the mike as if he were a nightclub stand-up, and started talking. *Quimp talking!* It stunned the audience. He announced that the character of Quimp—the name, costume, props, makeup style, and sketch material—would no longer be his property. He would choose a successor, and anybody who wanted to vie for the role could submit a check to him for two thousand dollars. Nonrefundable.''

"You make me sound like a flea marketeer," Spillman said. "I'm conducting an audition, not an auction. I am rigorously screening each person before awarding the title.''

"Let's see, four times two . . . eight thousand dollars. That's all?" I said.

"Those four over there are just the finalists," Jack said. "Lots more—fifteen, maybe twenty—paid the two thousand. You know how he narrowed it to four? They all wrote, in twenty-five words—"

"Twenty-five words or *less,*" Spillman said.

"Or less, the answer to this question: if Quimp weren't a clown, what would he do for a living? Harry, you're sitting beside the inventor, manager, *and* owner of the Yo-Yo Factory. He's tossing away a gold mine."

"First you call me a money-grubber, now a wastrel. Make up your mind, Jack. If you disapprove, why let us stay? I'm sure the Holiday Inn would take us."

"What happened to you, Marcus?" I said. "You always guarded your material more vigorously than corporations do their trademarks.''

He smiled the same infectious smile that had graced millions of cereal boxes. "The decision was spontaneous. When I grabbed that mike, I knew I'd say something important, but I didn't know what. However, it felt right then. And it still does now."

His obliqueness didn't surprise me. Spillman had written a book expounding his philosophies, an epigrammatic hodgepodge called *Clowning and Living.* It went unnoticed until the Zen Book Club made it an alternate selection, and its popularity snowballed. It inched onto best-seller lists and stayed for half a year. Just as people who had never jogged or fished read *The Complete Book of Running* and *The Compleat Angler,* most fans of *Clowning and Living* would never smear on clown white. Despite critics' howls, thousands found inspiration in such passages as: *"Onstage, the first ten laughs are for the dollars. The second ten repay the audience for those dollars. And the next five hundred? They're for the soul."*

Catapulted by the book, Spillman and his silent clown partner rode a crest of popularity that never subsided. Quimp did TV, the White House, and a one-man Broadway show—all without uttering a word. Quimp always let *Clowning and Living* talk for him. Up to now.

"You're quitting clowning altogether?" I asked.

"Absolutely."

"What will you do?"

"On my last visit to Vegas I went two days straight without sleep, watching the table magicians. No offense to you illusionists, but close-up is the real magic. I've decided to become a close-up man, eventually specializing in sleight of hand with playing cards."

His sense of timing was already flawless. He destroyed audiences with standard bits that most clowns got a mere chuckle with. I was sure he could become an average sleight-of-hand artist, but to rank with the best close-up men in the world was another matter. Although many of his clown routines used magic, they didn't come close to the subtle precision of the Vegas cardsharp. Most manipulative magicians begin practicing in their elementary school years, not in their forties. Spillman's career switch was the equivalent of a pro linebacker playing cello in a symphony orchestra. Although possible, success was astronomically improbable.

"Marcus, there's no guarantee, even with ten solid years of practice, you'll be good enough to play Vegas."

"In ten years I'll be fifty-four. Since I'm going to live to a hundred and five, that's still over fifty years of Vegas performing. I've already made progress. Watch."

He took out a half dollar and flip-flopped it across the back of his hand. He tried to make it vanish, but it bounced on the floor with the clinking noise ignominious to any sleight-of-hand man.

"Whoops. I'll try again."

Three more clinks, three more whoopses.

"Needs more work," he said. Red-faced, he pocketed the coin.

I offered to give Spillman pointers sometime, and he thanked me. Although I didn't use many in my act, I had learned basic sleights as a youngster and still practiced daily, as a relaxing ritual. They'd never earn me a Vegas close-up job, but that had never been my goal.

"Harry, besides Hodge, there's one more finalist you know," Spillman said.

I searched the group for another familiar face. Hodge was now sitting beside the last one still in makeup. The other two clowns were standing, engaged in a heated debate. The less verbal one was in his early thirties. He wore horn-rimmed glasses; his boyish looks were belied by his baldness. All that remained of his hairline was a brown wisp in front. On the sides, his hair swooped out in untamed waves, stopping just above his ears. I didn't know him.

When I asked, Jack told me he was a policeman from West Virginia.

"A cop who wants to be a clown?"

Jack said, "His name's Bill Rupeka, and he's on detached service from regular duty. Throughout West Virginia he hosts school assemblies with a crime-prevention theme. He hopes becoming the new Quimp will increase funding for his program."

Spillman said that Rupeka was the one with the rubber hammer who took charge in the office.

"The man Rupeka's talking to looks familiar, but I'm not sure if he's a magician," I said.

The man was twice Rupeka's age and had twice the hair. It was the color of dulled chrome. He was a Hollywood version of what we all wish we'd look like in late middle age: slender, tanned, with a worry-free, unlined face. When he talked, he made staccato gestures. His smile was warm but fleeting.

"He has the moves of a politician . . . or a preacher. Is he a gospel magician?" Gospel magicians used conjuring to illustrate religious lessons. My guess was ironic enough to make Jack chuckle.

"That is Lorenz Novak," Spillman said.

"Of course. I should have recognized him."

Novak wasn't a magician. A regular on national talk shows, he promoted a pet theory called Giggle Therapy. A giggle a day supposedly cured stress, high blood pressure, and a host of other ails—boffo health from boffo laughs.

Novak was a living legend. As the story goes, he developed his theory while fighting his way back from injuries thought to be fatal. Nowadays he often scorned and ridiculed the medical profession. In addition to his being a popular after-dinner speaker, his Health-Laugh seminars were constant sellouts.

I wondered if Novak took his own prescription. He always showed loads of comedy film clips at his seminars, but I was hard put to remember anything funny he ever said himself. A few years back we were both scheduled for the same TV talk show. When he learned he was bumped off the show because a comedian had run overtime, he smashed the green-room monitor with his shot glass of Scotch. He later blamed the broken glass on a child actor who also was waiting to go on.

"The Magicade booked Novak to lecture on 'Comedy and Health,'" Jack explained. "He talked about how entertainers, including magicians, actually help reduce illness in the world. I guess he thinks being the new Quimp will help his crusade."

Although Novak was a skilled speaker, I didn't think he had the makings of a clown. I couldn't see Spillman's reasoning in selecting him as a finalist.

"I wasn't sure if you knew Novak," Spillman said. "No, Harry, the clown you definitely know is *that* one."

Spillman pointed to the last one to remove makeup. With

his back to us, the clown pulled off his wig. Shoulder-length hair spilled down. A woman. She coaxed a comb through her hair. Jack and Spillman grinned when she faced us. She fluttered her fingers at me and then looked critically at herself in the mirror.

When she walked over, my dread and excitement must have shown. Spillman and Jack both tried and failed to suppress sly laughs. They probably believed in Guffaw Therapy: live longer by making asses of your friends.

This fourth clown was Cate Fleming, the only person I ever trusted to fire a .357 Magnum in my face.

CHAPTER FIVE

It had been five years since Cate and I last performed the Bullet-Catching Feat. We hadn't seen each other since parting, though her image was never far away. I had seen her aspirin commercials hundreds of times, and I often found her face smiling back at me from the clothing sections of mail-order catalogues. However, her passion was not for modeling, but for acting, and I didn't know how *that* career was faring.

"Harry, why are you here? Is this a convention of former magic greats?" She pinched my shirt at the shoulder, then kept her hand there. "Nice sweatshirt. Your assistant help pick the wardrobe?"

"I stopped using assistants. You were my last steady."

"I can't believe you've given up companionship on the road, or did you finally tire of treating assistants like your caged doves?"

I didn't have the heart to tell her about the doves.

"We're all in some kind of cage, Cate. But by the time we realize that we own both the lock *and* the key, it's usually too late to do anything about it."

Five years had changed her face in ways too subtle for a camera to pick up. Her eyes had lost some of their impishness, and she looked paler, though that could have been from the lack of makeup. Her baggy tramp costume kept me from ascertaining if she had lost weight.

I wanted to kiss her. Instead, I clasped her hand and shook it.

Three years ago, while waiting my turn in a hair salon, I noticed that the two women on either side of me clutched perfume ads torn from magazines. They starred Cate as a pouty seductress. Each woman intended to spend a small fortune to try to look like Cate. Even now, in her gaudy getup, I could see why.

"Wow! Harry Colderwood is now a one-man act. Hard to believe."

"Were you at Magicade as someone's assistant, Cate? Or are you a magician now?"

She thought that was funny. "I'm through with magic. This convention was just a lark. They've sent me invitations every year. The selection panel thinks you and I added new dimensions to the roles of magician and assistant. Rather than argue with poor judgment, I ignored the letters. Up until this year."

"Why the clown suit?"

"A challenge. Another role to win."

"Good luck. Clowning is not acting."

"I've heard that. Here's an even nastier rumor: they say you're doing trade shows."

"*Planning* to. Stanley Trimble is fronting me."

"You really want to shill customers for big business?"

"The businesses won't be big at first. Stanley's new at this game, too."

"Does he still drink?"

"I don't know."

"Better cash his checks fast."

"I do that with any check."

I asked how her husband was, and her face darkened. "Is he here?" I said. She shook her head no. "Does he still sell—what is it?—running shoes?"

"He's no salesman. He owns the company, and it manufactures exercise equipment." She opened and closed her raggedy clown coat, making a breeze. "Whew. It's getting hot. We'll have time to catch up later, Harry."

"Won't be a later. I'm already late for Allentown."

She shook her head. "Kowtowing to a manager. From Allentown, no less."

Two men, one wheeling a warehouse dolly, came through the front door and headed for the main desk. If not for their white smocks, I'd have thought they came from the trucking company to haul away more furniture. The one in front lifted the hinged counter so his partner could roll the dolly through. They knocked on the office door and were admitted. Before the door closed, I saw the office turn white from a camera flash.

Cate said, "Why don't you use that special magic wand I've read about and figure out who killed that poor schnook in the safe? You look surprised. Don't you think I read the papers?"

So she still felt I had treated her like a "piece of meat." But I knew The American Academy of Dramatic Arts didn't graduate pieces of meat.

"I'm good at reading *between* the lines, too. Especially those articles by that Gildea woman. I've often wondered: did you let her slip away?"

I nodded, trying to remember why I had let Cate go so easily, too.

"You're overestimating me," I said. "This case is out of my league. It has nothing to do with psychic phenomena or magic."

"No, Harry, you're wrong. At the Fitch, *everything* is magical."

The men in white emerged from the office, moving cautiously now. One walked backward, making sure the safe on the dolly didn't shift. The other one pushed, his face red with exertion.

The coroner and the sheriff came out. Standing with the deputy, they watched the attendants exit with their load. The coroner was a shrunken man with a pencil mustache and a face whose pinched wrinkles forced a constantly pained expression.

Hat in hand, Sheriff Virgil Tarrant spoke softly, at ease in front of a group. He was in his early fifties and wore his hair combed back and pressed flat. His receding hairline made his forehead seem huge, adding to his air of authority and intelligence. He carried a camera and a metal box that I guessed was an evidence-gathering kit. His uniform was at least a size too small, making me think he had recently gained weight. Tarrant's ill-fitting clothing was his only sloppiness. His tie, tie pin, badge, pocketful of pens, and leather holster all gave the effect of perfectly fitting puzzle pieces.

"We haven't identified the dead man yet," he said. "Nor will we speculate on cause of death before our coroner, Ted Crowell, performs an autopsy. If you know what rigor mortis is, I needn't explain why our first task will be to extricate the body from the safe." He gave Jack a wry smile. "You should have closed the place down when they wanted."

"No arguments from me, Virgil," Jack said.

"I'll be accompanying the coroner, but my deputy will stick around to take the remaining statements. For now, please stay in the hotel."

Trimble's going to love this, I thought.

Feeling like a student, I raised my hand. "Sheriff, I'm already late for a business engagement. Here's my manager's number where you can reach me if you have more questions."

He came over, took my slip of paper, and pocketed it. "You're staying like everyone else. I'll call your manager if you like, Mr. Colderwood. . . . Harry Colderwood. That name's familiar."

Before he could jog his memory, I said, "I don't want to trouble you. I'll call *you* when I get to Allentown."

Sheriff Tarrant sized me up like a boxer checking out an untested opponent. He smiled broadly, and I knew he'd decided it was heavyweight versus flyweight. "Ever serve on a jury, Colderwood?"

I shook my head.

"Everyone wants to be excused from jury duty. Few succeed. Why not view your stay here as a similar obligation? You'll reap the satisfaction of performing your civic duty.''

"What if I ignore you?"

"Then I'll consider you a fleeing suspect and put a slug in your ten-ring before you reach the door. Your head will look like an exploded watermelon.''

"With a Smith & Wesson .44 Special, you could do a lot of damage.''

He eyed me with grudging respect. "You know much about guns?''

"In my line of work, it pays to know a little about everything.''

"Just the same, try to leave and you'll be deader than that Bozo in the safe.''

I sighed, propped my feet up beside Jack's, and began sifting through the stacks of magazines.

Laymen. Every clown to them is a Bozo.

CHAPTER SIX

Jack and I shared a table in the barroom of the Fitch. Spillman and the clowns were now up in their rooms. It had been three hours since the sheriff's departure. Through the tinted door glass, I could see the deputy slumped on a lobby sofa, leafing through a *U.S. News and World Report*.

Ghostly shapes surrounded us—tables and chairs covered with sheets. Two Jack Daniel's bottles stood in the center of our table. The empty one held a burning candle. The other one was three-quarters full. The level of the whiskey was descending much faster than the level of the candle. The only other light was a flickering fluorescent tube behind the bar. Every now and then, Jack got up and slapped it on the side, stopping the blinking for a while.

Drinking, instead of easing the wait, only intensified my resentment of both the sheriff and Stanley Trimble. I had phoned the latter and explained my delay. He ranted, fearing some companies would object to their products' being associated with controversy. I told him that my stay here was involuntary. He called me a liar, fired me, hung up, and called back in three minutes to apologize, rehire me, and ask when I would arrive in Allentown. I told him I didn't know.

Jack said, "A hotel owner must accept inevitable unpleasantries: bar squabbles, heart attacks, suicides, lovers' spats turning violent. I felt lucky there was never a murder here."

"No one's calling it murder."

"We almost had one once. An anonymous phone caller told me that a husband intended to blow away the other two sides of a lovers' triangle who regularly rendezvoused at the Fitch. I called Sheriff Tarrant, and he intercepted the man's station wagon six blocks from here. The car was crammed with hunting gear—rifles, knives, and a foot-locker of ammo. Even bear traps. Who knows what they were for?"

"Tarrant's a good officer?"

"Sure, when it comes to routine matters—ticketing cars, controlling vandals, and locking up drunks. Plus he's always good for a favor or two."

His voice rose, tilting the candle flame toward me. "But Tarrant needs outside help on this. Maybe he's worried about reelection. Maybe he wants to land a better job somewhere else. Regardless of why, he's going to screw this up if he insists on shouldering this murder case alone."

"Who says it's murder?"

He drained his glass and thudded it down on the table. "Damn, I hate being forced out of business, but at least I thought I'd exit clean. Now, instead of being remembered for magic, the Fitch will go down as the place where clowns came to be murdered. *Nobody* staying here can afford having his name mixed up in this."

"I agree."

"Do you think Tarrant can even properly identify the body?"

"Jack, don't get carried away. We didn't leave our pieces at the Fitch for nothing. No one will forget what this place meant."

Pieces was slang for the memorabilia and souvenirs we magicians left behind. It was a tradition: visit the Fitch and leave a piece. As the collection grew, Jack relegated most of it to a basement storage room, keeping the best posters and photos for display in the restaurant and bar. Nobody knew exactly what all was down there, or how much it was worth.

"Our friend in the safe turned out to be the dandiest piece of them all," Jack said.

I freshened his drink.

He continued. "My new apartment will seem like a pup tent after living in this place, and I'll spend my last days with an unsolved killing hanging over me. Why did I let Spillman talk me into staying open?"

He kept his eyes fixed on me while tilting his head back to drink. He glared at me the way a child might when tactlessly hinting for an allowance hike. I hoped I was misreading him.

Don't ask me to do it, Jack.

"So I can drop you a line, what's your new address, Jack?"

He spat out his words. "You've got to help me, Harry. How much do you want? Three thousand? That would buy a lot of tricks for your tour."

"Jack, don't believe the newspapers. I'm an entertainer, nothing else. I *create* illusion; I don't dispel it. You're underestimating Tarrant. He might clear this up fast."

"You're modest. What about that Baltimore wife-killer? You cracked that one."

"I didn't really solve it. I just proved the plausibility of my theory. An unknown assailant had strangled a woman to death in Severna Park. Police suspected her ex-husband, but he had an alibi: he was sleeping it off in a drunk tank in Baltimore."

"He was an escape artist, right?"

"Almost. His uncle was a technical consultant during the thirties for Hardeen, Harry Houdini's brother. I demonstrated that a man with a knowledge of escapology could slip out of that jail, drive to Severna Park, and return in time to finish slumbering with the winos. After the police saw that possibility, they uncovered the Hardeen connection."

"I heard you couldn't resist the theatrics."

"I guess not. The chief of police thought his jail was escape-proof. I posed as a wino (a depressingly easy task) and got arrested. I picked my way out of jail, stole the chief's family car, and drove to Severna Park. I parked in front of the murder victim's house, returned in a rental, and broke back into jail long before the first drunk stirred.

"They were processing me out when the chief showed up late for work. Grumbling, he started to file a stolen-car report. His spirits plummeted totally when I handed him his keys. The rest is history."

No longer paying attention to me, Jack stared into his glass. "Is five thousand dollars sweet enough? Your van needs work."

"Save your money for retirement. I don't need it."

"You do. I mean *did*. Figuring you'd balk, I've already given it to you. Indirectly."

"What?"

"I called your manager an hour ago, when you were talking to the deputy. Trimble said you guys need backing, or you won't get ten miles out of Allentown."

"What do you mean I've already *got* the money?"

"I authorized my accountant to release a cashier's check for five thousand. It's on its way to Trimble. Anonymously."

"Guilt won't work, Jack. You just lost five big ones, you sly bastard. Refunds, as well as telling the truth, are against Trimble's religion. He won't admit even receiving it. In case you've forgotten, *this* is what I do for a living."

I proffered my empty hands. A spark zipped between them. I made loose fists, and tinsel strips spiraled from both, continuing for a half minute, leaving two mounds of glinting foil on the table.

"Good trick," he said, pretending indifference. "But I heard Al Goshman does it better."

He dropped a room key atop the cushion of tinfoil.

"You can stay in 206 while working on the case," he said. "We've carted the furniture out of all the other rooms. I hope it won't embarrass you, being right next to Cate Fleming." His smile was devious.

"No way am I going to—"

The deputy stuck his head in. "Phone call, Mr. O'Connell."

I picked up the key as Jack went out to the lobby phone. Too late to hit the highway now, I thought. A room's better than sleeping in the van.

I got up and looked at the framed posters on the wall. Most were the same as the last time I had visited the Fitch: Carter the Great beating the Devil at cards, Harry Houdini when he was still billing himself the King of Cards, and a blindfolded Karl Germain writing people's thoughts on a chalkboard.

At the bar, I searched in vain for the electromagnet a former bartender/magician once used for a spirit trick.

When Jack returned, his walk was energetic.

"Case closed, Harry. All over. Don't try returning the five thousand. Consider it thanks for the good times you've brought the Fitch."

"Who'd you talk to, Jack? The sheriff?"

"The dead man has been identified as Perry Vaughn. A local punk, a real troublemaker whose name was always in the paper for fights and disturbances. He busted up a lot of bars, but thank God he never hung out at the Fitch. Maybe all the magic scared him away. It was a matter of time before he'd wind up behind bars—or dead."

"Spillman said the clowns began today at five A.M. Why did Vaughn take such a risk? Why not break in earlier, wearing comfortable street clothes instead of a costume? His makeup was one-hundred-percent professional. Do you know if Vaughn was connected with entertainment?"

Jack fumbled putting the cap back on the whiskey. "It's not worth worrying over, Harry. How about some coffee for the road? What's your favorite? Regular or decaf?"

I pocketed the room key. Jack swallowed hard.

"I'm sticking around after all, Jack. Just to learn who Marcus picks as the new Quimp. No other reason, mind you. Oh, I might coach Cate if she's dead serious about winning the competition. Thanks for the five thousand, too.

I lied. We desperately need cash. I'll repay you. Somehow. Sometime."

I scooped up the tinsel coils, but Jack forced my hands onto the table. He leaned close.

"The case is solved, Harry. Solved. Everybody here will be happy if it stays solved. You're not considering actually *earning* that five grand, are you?"

I slipped out of his grip and interlocked my fingers. Smoke rose from my hands, making Jack cough.

"See? I'm a magician, Jack. An entertainer. Nothing else. I live for footlights and applause."

"You're not very convincing. Oh, Jesus, do you have to smile like that?"

"Think I'll turn in early," I said and yawned. "Big day tomorrow. If you need me, I'll be in 206. Next to Cate."

Jack sank into his chair, shoving the tinsel off the table. He opened his bottle and poured a long one.

On my way out, he mumbled something about having created a monster.

CHAPTER SEVEN

Cleaning up the Think-A-Drink mess was a hands-and-knees job, and I was glad the liquid hadn't ruined any other tricks. I didn't want my equipment smelling like whiskey for my next children's show. I checked along the van floor for glass. Each chunk I found I dropped in a plastic garbage bag. I nicked myself on a sliver and cursed the dim lighting.

I could hear the clank and thrash of the garment factory two blocks away. Since few cars now used the street in front of the hotel, all traffic noises were distant. I tried to recall what buildings used to flank the Fitch, but my memory was fuzzy. An ethnic food market on the left. A church on the right. Or was that a liquor store? The closest building now was five lots down—the Edison Office Building, with its glassless windows. The rest of the block was bulldozed mud.

I bagged the last of the glass, sucked on my hurt finger, and tried picturing Perry Vaughn in the predawn, slinking down this street in full Quimp regalia. The image refused to play.

Footsteps broke my reverie.

They halted at the open doors at the back of my van. Streetlights from behind gave the man a dark outline. He wore a cowboy hat.

"Everything okay?" the silhouette asked.

"Just tidying up. Calling it a night, Deputy Wirfel?"

He removed his hat, rubbed a palm over the top of his

head and down the back of his neck, then put his hat back on.

"Yeah, I'm heading out. Whew! It smells in here. You having a party?"

I jangled the bag of glass and explained to him about Think-A-Drink. "Just a few puddles to sop up now."

Wirfel stepped inside and was no longer a silhouette. His face was gritty, overdue for a shave. The knot of his tie drooped two inches below his collar button. He sat on the edge of a trunk and groaned. I wondered what he wanted.

Wirfel eyed the trunks stacked along the sides of the van. The only clues that my cargo was a magic show were my disassembled guillotine and a straitjacket that, along with Think-A-Drink, I had been too lazy to pack properly.

I said, "Looks like a torture chamber, doesn't it? That guillotine stands ten feet high when put together, and it shocks the hell out of the audience when the blade passes through the volunteer's neck without harm. My routine is for laughs, but since I started using it, I get paid quicker."

"You do escapes?" he said, fingering the sleeve of the straitjacket beside him.

"Nah. That's my smoking jacket. Very comfortable."

I tore off six feet of paper towel and worked on the pools of Jack Daniel's, guaranteeing myself clear sinuses for the rest of the night.

"I wanted to see you before you moved on. Dr. Crowell's completed the preliminary autopsy, but there'll be the usual ten-day wait for the toxicology and other lab reports. If you want, I'll drop you a line when they come back."

"I appreciate that. You're Tarrant's only deputy?"

"No, we have a night man who helps out. But frankly, he doesn't take his job seriously."

I tossed the soaked wad of towel into the garbage bag and attacked the last damp spots with a new towel.

Wirfel went on. "Sheriff Tarrant's a stickler for detail. He takes reams of notes on every case. His thoroughness has put a lot of guilty men out of commission. I know you thought he was rude, but he was only doing his job. Take your job, for instance. What do you do if someone in the audience heckles you? I'll bet you don't ignore him.''

"No, but I don't threaten to blow his head off, either. Tell Tarrant that that style of smoking jacket comes in a variety of sizes.''

"Vaughn was trying to rip off the hotel. He was carrying burglar tools. The coroner says there were bruises and abrasions on his hands, which supports the theory he was locked in that safe alive. He probably panicked and clawed the inside of the safe until he passed out.''

"Nifty way to go." I put a twist-tie on the bag, then moved up to the driver's seat. I started the van.

Wirfel jumped to his feet. "Whoa, wait. Don't want a stowaway, do you?''

I manhandled the shift into reverse and touched the gas. The front tire rolled off the curb, bouncing the trunks and the deputy. He jutted out both arms to the sides of the van to keep balance. I shifted to neutral, tromped the gas, pulled on the emergency brake, and killed the engine.

Both arms still against the walls, Wirfel looked at me with new awe and said, "You're staying?''

"Yeah.''

"Only overnight, right?''

"Maybe more. Think Jack's taken HBO out of the rooms yet?'' I got out and slammed the door.

He caught up with me at the hotel entrance.

"Do you know what you're getting into?''

"Yes, and it doesn't have anything to do with Perry Vaughn. I'm just taking a short vacation.''

"In a hotel that's days away from demolition?''

"I'll be in number 206 if you or Tarrant wants me.''

He leaned on the door to prevent my entering.

"Goddammit, Colderwood. It all went down the way Tarrant says it did.'' Wirfel was so close, the brim of his hat touched my forehead.

"It did? Then what was Vaughn trying to steal? Money?

The restaurant and bar are both closed down. There are no new guests. All the clown contestants are staying for free. Where was the cash?''

"Jack O'Connell said that yesterday he deposited the rest of the money from the convention. He was late because the pressures of closing the hotel have him off-balance. Vaughn probably thought the money was still in the Fitch.''

"What did Vaughn do for a living?''

"Nothing. No trade. The only thing he was skilled at was inflicting pain. He was such a bum, he was even too lazy to drift from town to town.''

"Like I do?''

"No comment.''

"How old was he?''

"Twenty-seven, born in Roselle. He and I went to high school together. Both his parents died the same year he dropped out.''

"Natural causes?''

"Yes, although some say nothing was natural when it came to Vaughn. He's been giving Tarrant grief as long as I can remember. Thank God, Tarrant always handled him. I'm not ashamed to say I was scared of Vaughn; nor am I ashamed to say good riddance.''

"Was Vaughn an entertainer?''

"Yeah. He had a one-man audience—himself. Whatever he wanted, he took—the easiest way he knew. He lived with his girl friend, Michelle Blue, but it's unlikely there was much love there. The only one Vaughn respected was Sheriff Tarrant, who busted his chops every chance he got. No, Vaughn was no entertainer in the conventional sense.''

"Why the clown makeup?''

"The goings-on at the Magicade were no secret. It was town news, including Marcus Spillman's announcement to select a successor. We figure he knew there'd be a lot of people here wearing Quimp makeup. Spillman's such a kook, who knows what hours they'd be keeping? Not knowing when it would be safe to sneak into the hotel to rob it, a clown suit was a perfect disguise. Vaughn could have hired someone to make him up.''

"That makeup was professional. Who around here is that good?''

"I'm not at liberty to say. Listen, Vaughn broke in intending to steal whatever he could lay his mitts on, and he blew it. Want to see where he pried open the conference-room window? Jack O'Connell told us that his safe was definitely unlocked at one A.M. when he went up to his personal suite to go to bed. Allison King was at the desk since seven this morning, and she said that no one without a clown suit, except Spillman, entered that office.''

I didn't tell him Allison was asleep when I showed up. I took out a notepad and wrote down "Michelle Blue." Wirfel frowned when I drew a question mark beside her name. I said, "Any secondary theories?''

"Of course, drugs could have triggered Vaughn's behavior. The toxicology reports will tell us if narcotics were in his system.''

"You'll have to do better than that.''

He didn't. As he still refused to budge, I sidestepped, using the revolving door.

I pushed hard in case he tried to block it. Inside, I turned around and watched his lips move, stringing together profanities.

In the second-floor hallway, Bill Rupeka was sitting spread-eagle, back to the wall. He worked his deck of playing cards with the contented repetition of an old woman knitting.

He wore gym shorts and a plaid sports shirt. He had on a thick headband made from a red polka-dot handkerchief.

"Working on your sidesteal?" I asked.

"If you know it's a sidesteal, I must be doing it shitty.''

"Not that bad." I reached out, and he gave me the cards. "You're flashing from this angle. See? A ten-degree tilt of your right hand should correct it. Also, the deck is talking when you palm out the card. Not much, but I could hear it click. Concentrate on relaxing all your fingers."

He let me demonstrate twice, but no more. I returned the cards, and he attacked them with determination. Fumbling at first, he began improving on the tenth try.

"Jack putting you up for the night?" he said, keeping his eyes on his hands.

"Yeah."

Rupeka plugged away, striving for perfection. Fatigue set in somewhere past try number fifty, and he started dropping cards. Finally the whole deck flew from his grip. He tried restacking the deck, but his hands were numb and cards slipped away. He laughed, opening and closing his hands to work out the stiffness.

He said, "When's your next TV show? I just got a video recorder, and I could learn a lot watching you over and over on tape."

I forced a smile, as always when that question arose. "Don't hold your breath."

"Is it true what they say? That the networks have blackballed you because of that fortune-teller incident?"

"Don't believe all you hear."

But he was right. Five years ago I had learned from a tipster that the network had, on the advice of a payrolled analyst, postponed airing my special. This "expert" was a psychic who used tea leaves, a crystal ball, and a tarot deck to advise the network on key programming decisions. I went public with the scandal, but the public didn't care. However, the networks did.

They branded me a troublemaker. My TV days were over, and my salad days were just beginning. I was still a salad-eater today. I should consider trade shows a step up, but working with Stanley Trimble made it a sideways move at best.

Rupeka inserted a cigarette in the corner of his mouth, but wouldn't let me light it. He gently cracked his knuckles and massaged his fingers.

"You handle the pasteboards well. Why try to be a clown?" I asked.

"I already *am* a clown—as well as a magician."

I was going to say that he had more natural sleight-of-hand skill than Spillman—until I saw the copy of *Clowning and Living* on the floor beside him. Spillman's signature was on the cover. His mentor?

"You think a lot of Spillman?" I asked.

"No, but I admire Quimp."

I was glad someone else distinguished between the two.

"This is my third copy of his book; I wore out the others. This contest is a dream come true."

"Quite a leap, isn't it? Cop to clown?"

"Not at all. I'm still a policeman, but now I'm working more on prevention than on cure. My school assemblies combine magic, clowning, and low-key brainwashing."

"Think it would have made a difference if Perry Vaughn had seen an assembly show like yours when he was a kid?"

Rupeka sucked on his unlit cigarette, looking at me as if I were a smartass punk who had run a red light.

"Vaughn was the name of the guy in the safe," I said.

I started to update him, but he waved me into silence. He resumed practicing, but his finesse was gone, and he bent several cards. Instead of stopping, he tightened his grip and continued fanatically.

"The sheriff says Vaughn died accidentally during a burglary attempt. You buy that?" I said.

Rupeka shrugged. More cards slopped to the floor.

"Bill, if this were your case, what would you think?"

The rest of the deck squirted from his hands. He scooped them up, missing several. He jammed them into Quimp's book, squeezed it shut, and stood up.

"Good night, Mr. Colderwood."

Playing cards slid out of the book and fluttered to the floor.

"I want your professional opinion. Please. It's important."

"All right," he replied dryly, taking the cigarette from his lips.

A hell of a way to quit smoking, walking around with an unlit cigarette, I thought. Almost self-torture. I lit one of my own, but it didn't tempt him to do likewise.

"Before a show, do you get a kick out of some local amateur fiddling with your equipment or giving unsolicited pointers?"

Before I could reply, he said, "I didn't think so. For your information, Sheriff Tarrant asked if I wanted in on this one, and I politely declined. You want my professional opinion? Bug off, Colderwood. When it comes to police work, you're nothing but an unwanted amateur. Don't even unpack your bag. Quit worrying about scum like Vaughn, and get your ass out of here." He slammed his door behind him.

I picked up the stray cards and stacked them by his door. At three A.M., after tossing and turning, he'd come out for his inevitable walk-and-a-smoke (real smoke this time, I bet). Then he could retrieve the cards.

At high volume, Carson's monologue and laughter wafted from under Rupeka's door. I passed the next room and heard laughter coming from it, too—along with some Amos-and-Andy dialogue, followed by a few Benny lines, and then an exchange of insults between McCarthy and Fields: a collection of classic radio comedy. Novak's room.

I listened for Novak's laughter amid the canned chuckles. None. Either great comedy put Novak to sleep, or my suspicions were true: he had a hell of time practicing what he preached. I waited a few minutes in hopes of hearing some Lenny Bruce. No such luck.

From the next room, I heard the clink of a dropped coin. Silence. Then more clinking. No swearing, though. I admired Spillman's patience.

The occupant of the room beside Spillman's was snoring with abandon. It was Gregory Hodge, the magic collector, probably dreaming of the next addition to his holdings.

Cate's room, 204, was next. I passed, trying not to listen. *That* would have been eavesdropping. I considered all my previous nosiness as legitimate investigation. To get any sleep at all the next few days, I'd have to continue making such subtle distinctions.

My key was in my door when I heard an eggbeater-like whirring coming from her room. I walked back to her door. Besides the whirr, there was also dance music. I put my ear to the door so I could, uh, investigate better.

I wanted to knock, but what would I say? How about: *Hi, this is your former employer and lover, and I dropped by to show you this enormous torch I'm carrying. It's burning the hell out of my fingers. Mind if I set it down and drop in for a while? And not leave for a couple weeks? By the way, what was that whirring noise?*

Jimbo's Pizza came to my rescue. I smelled the pepperoni before I spotted the deliveryman. He tromped through the stairwell door, carrying a box and a paper bag. Paper hat damp with sweat, he checked his watch twice on the way up the hall.

Panting, he said, "Damn elevator. It's been working all week. Glad it's not the fifth floor tonight. You order the pie?"

"For 204?"

He gave an exhausted nod, and I paid for the pie. Then I dickered for his paper hat.

I ended up eating most of the pizza. When Cate polished off her last slice, she said, "You didn't have to do an impersonation to come in and visit."

I took off the pizza hat and threw it away. "I didn't want to appear nosy, but I had to know what that whirring was."

"Satisified?"

"Partly. I'm sure your husband knows the exercise equipment business, but I can't see a market for portable exercise bikes for travelers."

She again mounted her bike and moved her legs up and down. The wheel spun, but she traveled nowhere. She reminded me of a Judy Garland in tights, furiously pedaling to save Toto.

I said, "The real exercise would be lugging that thing through airports. By the way, if you eat pizza after every session with the bike, won't that counteract the benefits? Your husband might decide to drop you from the promotional ads."

"I don't do any ads for Phil. He and I agreed it wouldn't be ethical. Would you consider doing some? We're looking for before-and-after shots."

I didn't ask which category I belonged in. I took out a cigarette.

"Don't even *think* about lighting that. I can't tolerate smoke anymore. Phil won't even hire smokers. He offers bonuses for those who lose weight and participate in sports like racquetball or marathoning."

Would my seducing Cate be a sport, Phil, old boy? Do you offer a bonus for that?

"You'll feel better if you quit," she said. "I know I did."

"I don't have the incentive."

"You always were big on incentives. There must be a whopper of a goody bag to keep you here at the Fitch."

"I'm not as greedy as you think. Some things I do for no profit motive. Just for the hell of it. I could stop smoking this very minute, but I don't really want to." Familiar, fatal words.

"Let me know when. This I gotta see."

She got off her bike, inspected the empty pizza box for stray cheese, then stuffed it in the waste can.

"When did you meet your husband?" I asked.

"About four years ago, while working for a summer theatre near Boston. We were doing a stage version of one of those Hollywood beach movies, and the director didn't like the way the actors looked without shirts on. He rented exercise equipment from Phil's company, despite Phil's arguments that a few weeks of exercise weren't going to make much difference in their appearance. When the equipment arrived, so did Phil. He watched one rehearsal and asked to be introduced to me.''

That was her version. In reality, she probably met him like she met me—a calculated accident. I had just finished doing a local talk show in Minneapolis when a woman introduced herself as Cate Elliott. She critiqued my performance more thoroughly and harshly than any professional critic ever had. Until the director threw her out of the studio, I thought she was a station employee. She was, instead, a local aspiring actress who had bluffed her way into meeting someone who might help her career. I hired her.

"You weren't surprised to see me knocking at your door," I said.

"I *know* you."

She tugged at the loose areas of her exercise outfit. Sky-blue, it flattered the places most women worry over. Its delightful illusion of transparency would have stimulated most men's imaginations. For me, it stimulated memory.

Using the room's desk as a dancer's bar, she coaxed her limbs into seemingly life-threatening stretch positions. Her honey-colored hair covered her eyes, and she didn't bother to push it away.

"You glad I stayed?" I asked.

"Not really. I can't do two jobs at once."

She was several steps ahead of me.

"How's that?" I said.

"It may seem petty to you, but this competition's important. Winning would get me national attention. Right now these auditions are requiring everything I know about acting—and then some. I'm not going to wreck my concentration by scouring the countryside for clues to what may not even be a crime."

First the paper hat. Now this. More bargaining. I said, "I've seen all Quimp's routines at least ten times. I know how his mind works. I too am a professional entertainer. And I spent two summers as an apprentice clown for a one-ring, patched-tent circus. I also know the strengths and weaknesses of the other competitors. Not one of them has a coach or a director. Except you.''

"Oh, are you applying for the job?"

"Do I need references?"

"No, you're hired. With no strings attached, right?"

"Wrong."

I explained the strings. She listened passively and then consented. Then, because it was one of the strings, she told me what she knew about the day's events.

She didn't recall seeing anyone in costume behaving oddly. She never saw more than three other clowns at once. When Allison discovered the body, all the clowns were in the conference room, each ready to demonstrate his rendition of Quimp's Milk Routine, where milk repeatedly appears and vanishes, finally spouting from the clown's elbow.

"Now your end of the bargain," she said.

Stifling yawns, I guided Cate step by step through Quimp's Peekaboo Entrance, where the curtain viciously attacks him each time he sashays onstage. She used the window drape as a stage curtain. Her rapid learning and willing acceptance of direction impressed me, but she beat me to the compliment.

"You've acquired patience," she said. "Your bad temper was one reason I left you. It was usually worst after we'd discuss my acting goals. Also, I hated the loneliness. When I first met Phil, he made me feel I belonged in his life, but now he acts as though I'm another low-priority item. He's put me on the back burner as if I were a fizzling business deal. Harry, I think Phil is a magician too, but a different kind. He certainly fooled me. I guess I'll never be a good magic audience. Getting fooled hurts."

She remounted her rickety bike. I tried telling her she was a glutton for punishment, but my words slurred. The clacking bike drowned out my other snide comments. The Fleming Porto-Bike came equipped with a speedometer that measured how many fake miles per hour she was doing on the fake roadways. The bike shimmied. I assumed it was now simulating a jaunt down a pothole-infested country lane.

The room gradually turned gelatinous, its quivering expansion and contraction a result of too little sleep and too much pizza, mixed with a good dose of dread. And those hours of practicing Think-A-Drink.

I turned on the dance music tape and fell asleep. Still on the chair, I awoke three hours later, vaguely remembering Cate kissing me good night. Or was it a dream?

Walking softly so as not to wake her, I reluctantly left her room, which smelled of perfume, bike-chain oil, and stage makeup. I went to 206 and unpacked.

No longer sleepy.

Three A.M.

CHAPTER EIGHT

Four A.M.

As I watched from my window, a pickup pulled in front of the hotel, and with Sheriff Tarrant overseeing, two men heaved and hoed the safe back inside. Why return it at this hour?

From elsewhere in the building, I heard clanking pipes, rushing water, and a radio show featuring a morning man who thought he was a riot.

The hiss of the shower stopped, and I heard someone singing a marching tune. The singer did impressions of both brass and percussion instruments. Spillman. I wished he would shower in pantomime.

Wearing only trousers, I lay back down and laced my fingers behind my head, knowing that sleep was impossible.

I thought of Perry Vaughn being locked in that safe. I've been locked up before—mostly in the name of entertainment, but a few times in the name of the law. Twice (charges later dropped) for disorderly conduct, venting anger in antisocial ways toward former managers. The cops knew that locking me up was largely a symbolic gesture, and I never tried to escape. Also a symbolic gesture.

Too lazy to find a clean shirt, I put on my sweatshirt. I thought again about the safe and decided to let experience be the best teacher.

The sheriff had locked Jack's office. A minor delay. I picked the lock. Once inside, I saw they had put the safe a few feet to the left of its original spot. A chalk-line rectangle around the former location mocked the practice of outlining the spot where a corpse had lain. Dark humor or investigative procedure carried to ridiculous extremes?

I clicked on the desk lamp, then tapped the walls and peered behind picture frames and the bookcase. No secret panels, I thought, smiling.

Satisfied that the only entrances to the office were from the lobby and the conference room, I filled my chest with cigar-tainted air and took on the safe.

The door was ajar, so I didn't have to play safecracker. I opened it wide.

Empty. No hand fell out. No glassy-eyed corpse. Sorry folks, fresh out of dead bodies today.

Its sleek, black interior reeked of cleanser, courtesy of the Virgil Tarrant Janitorial Service—Evidence Scoured While-U-Wait.

I crawled inside.

I don't always rush in where angels fear to stoop and crawl. If I weren't alone, sleepless, and a victim of too much bad pizza, I wouldn't have been caught dead—I mean alive—in that metal box.

It was only after I got comfy that some bastard locked me in. He slammed the door and spun the combination knob.

All my escapology training paid off. I handled myself calmly and rationally. For a while.

Slow breathing. Must conserve air.

I had never done an escape from a safe. I tried to utilize what I had read on the subject, but I couldn't. It was like trying to cook a meal relying solely on a ten-year-old memory of a recipe.

Slow breathing. No panic.

I did fine until I realized that my knees were so close to my chest that I couldn't take even half a normal breath. I did the most logical thing: I panicked, pummeling my fists on the door.

I began spouting nonsense, beseeching the gods for intervention. None showed up. They were probably snickering, remembering all my crusades against spiritualism and superstition.

I heard singing: "Forty to the left. Twenty-six to the right. Thirty-seven to the left. You do the hucklebuckle, and you shake it all around. That's what it's all about!"

Thunk.

The door swung open, and the office lights burned my eyes.

Jack O'Connell's head filled the opening of the safe. Kneeling, he shoved a pistol in my face and kept it there until he recognized me.

"That's how you remember the combination?" I asked. "You sing the Bunny Hop song?" My heart still roared like a lawn mower.

"Yep. It works sometimes. I couldn't find that card with the combination on it. Tarrant must still have it. I heard you repeating someone's name over and over. Who's Zeek?"

"No, Zeus. Among others. Zeus was the supreme god of the Greeks. Do me a favor. Don't tell anyone. I've got a reputation to protect."

He lowered the pistol and helped me out. He wore blue-and-gold paisley pajamas. "I woke you? I must have been noisier than I thought," I said.

"No, I was sound asleep. You weren't really noisy. You forget: I'm the innkeeper. Weird sounds always wake me."

"How much noise do you think Vaughn made prying open the conference-room window?"

Already we were shooting holes in the Vaughn-as-burglar theory . . . unless *Jack* was the one who had closed the final steel-plated chapter of Vaughn's life. If so, I was a luckier man than I thought.

By Zeus.

CHAPTER NINE

Railroad tracks divided Roselle in half. To cross town, drivers used any one of four bridges. The bridges were also handy places for passing motorists to dispose of litter. Good thing the tracks were in disuse. Otherwise, the heaps of garbage would have derailed any train foolish enough to venture through Roselle. I didn't know which side of the tracks constituted the "good" side, but apparently it wasn't the Fitch's, since its block was the first doomed to dubious redevelopment.

Safety might not have been the sole reason Roselle posted a severely reduced speed limit on the highway through town. Perhaps the municipal council envied all the smiles on the out-of-town drivers passing through. Creeping through Roselle at twenty-miles-per would now be enough to erase anyone's smile.

Roselle could no longer appear and disappear in a wink for highway travelers. They could no longer ignore the endless blocks of bars, churches, and lunch counters. I wasn't sure in what category Murray's Bar and Grill was; it was a curious mixture of all three.

Murray's had no menus. A blackboard announced the daily fare, but listed no prices. When it came time to pay, Murray, a flower-pot-shaped man in a yellowed apron, would gaze at the items on the check and suggest what he thought was a fair price. His quick-estimate system was an apparent success. The place was overflowing for breakfast.

All the food smelled like bacon. Cutting across that was

a heavier odor of beer. The crowd was mostly highway road-workers decked out in wrinkled work suits and caps bearing sports and liquor insignias. Loud-talking, sports-coated salesmen were an additional part of Murray's morning scene.

Most of the customers had heard about Perry Vaughn. Just as Tarrant had promised, the morning paper carried a two-line obit with no details about a safe or a clown suit. One old-timer offered to buy me breakfast if I had anything to do with Vaughn's death. A party atmosphere reigned, but I couldn't get any of the celebrants to regale me with stories about Perry Vaughn. For that I had to venture to the darker side of Murray's—the bar.

A wall with an archway separated the two sections. The bar was lined with somber, slouched figures—Murray's other seven A.M. crowd. I used liquid currency as my introduction, and the patrons cheerfully gave me the rundown on Vaughn. That's precisely what they did. Run him down.

Including one elderly gent wearing a bow tie. Beside him on the floor was a fiddle, his prize possession. His name, Cal, was printed on the burgundy case. When I called it a violin instead of a fiddle, he chewed me out. After tossing down the shot and half the beer I bought him, Cal told me what Vaughn had done to him.

Two weeks earlier Vaughn had staggered into Murray's. The bartender refused to serve him and got a forearm smash on the ear for his impertinence.

"Nobody came to his aid?" I asked.

"Look around," Cal said. "Social Security's picking up this bar's tab. See any heroes drinking here? Besides, Perry-boy was quick, and he wrote the book on dirty fighting. Never heard of him losing. I once heard he enrolled in a karate school, and on the first night of class, he broke the teacher's arm in three places. He put his fist through the wall and asked who was next. The school closed a few weeks later."

Cal raised his half-glass of beer and didn't lower it until he had reduced the contents to foam. The bartender caught

my nod and gave him a fresh setup. "I used to play fiddle
every day, but now with arthritis I can't play worth a damn
some days. After smacking the barkeep, Vaughn wanted
music—*live* music. I refused, but finally played when he
threatened to stomp my fiddle. Ain't no Stradivarius, but
it's the last one I'll ever own. I serenaded that sonofabitch
until he got bored. He called my music stupid, poured beer
in my empty case, and moved on. Humiliating."

"Vaughn have many friends?"

"None. Used to have a few cronies, but they deserted
him when they found out he could turn on them as fast as
a Doberman who's missed feeding time. Had a girl friend,
though—name of Michelle Blue. I heard she's a zero, but
common sense tells you she'd have to be."

For the next hour, I sipped coffee while he drank boil-
ermakers and told me more Perry Vaughn tales. They all
blended into one humorless saga of violence, vandalism,
and thievery. He said Vaughn had no job, that he was a
"professional slime."

"Sheriff Tarrant was the only person that seemed to have
a hold over Vaughn, but the law now is different than in
my day. That's why Virgil Tarrant could never put him
away for long. Lately, Vaughn was starting to bad-mouth
even Tarrant, saying how no one could stop him."

Cal asked around the bar and came up with Michelle
Blue's address. He got his colleagues to raise their glasses
in unison, in commemoration of Vaughn's demise.

"How are the fingers today?" I asked.

He didn't need coaxing. He got out his fiddle and played
"For He's a Jolly Good Fellow." The bartender turned off
the TV, and all joined in the singing. Even some of Murray's grill crowd drifted over into the beery dimness.

They were on the sixth verse when I left. I love holidays.

There was a yard sale at Michelle Blue's. Pickup trucks
lined the street, forcing me to park down the block.

Standing at a card table, a young woman haggled with
customers and took their cash. She told me she was a friend

of Michelle's and directed me inside. The house was a duplex, and it looked as though the tenant of each half was battling to see who could first plunge the structure into oblivion.

I pounded the front door lightly. Hard knocking would have jarred loose its cracked glass. No answer, so I walked in.

Michelle Blue was in the living room. Hands on hips, she was arguing with a boy wearing a high school band jacket. She wore running shorts with the sides slit nearly to the waistband. The more she peppered her speech with profanity, the more flustered the kid got. "Cash only," she said. "Though if you come back in two years, I might consider another form of payment."

Instead of a coffee table, a CX 500 custom Honda stood in front of the couch. The boy wanted to buy the bike.

I cleared my throat, and her head snapped around. She warned me not to spit on the rug.

"What are you? Cop, customer, or insurance man?"

I said, "Insurance." I doubted that Vaughn had an insurance man. But if he did, he would probably have been dressed like me: hooded jacket, turtleneck, cords, and a pair of moccasin loafers with toes skinned raw.

She said, "With this yard sale on top of everything else, things have been hectic. I took time to check his policy this morning. I think I'm entitled to double indemnity."

"We'll iron out the details later. I've got some questions first. Only a formality, you understand."

"Christ, I *knew* it. Even from the grave, Perry Vaughn is going to fuck me over." She turned to the boy. "Go home and get your old man. If he looks honest like you, I'll take a check. If he's as cute as you, I'll tell him to stick around while you ride the bike home."

The boy tried to leave in a hurry, but he couldn't get the screen door open. She worked it for him, putting her hand through the ripped screen and twisting the outside handle.

"Now, Mr. Insurance, ask away."

Michelle Blue's T-shirt was a double ad. It proclaimed

the name of a fitness spa, and it also showcased her ample physique. She brushed against me, providing a lingering sample of both softness and hardness. She told me she was an instructor at the spa whose name was printed across her chest.

"Do you carry any Fleming exercise equipment at your spa?"

"Are you kidding?" she said. "Phil Fleming's a first-class worm. His company never did repair the shoddy crap they sold us. Now that he's ruined himself in the spa market, I hear he's trying to develop portable equipment for consumers. Probably junk, too."

I looked at the For Sale sign dangling from the motor-cycle handlebars and said, "You're liquidating Mr. Vaughn's assets already? Your enterprise is astonishing."

"A coincidence. I ran ads for this sale all last week. So I couldn't call it off. Yard-sale folks are like junkies."

Starting with innocuous questions about age and occupation, I learned that Vaughn's last job had been two years ago at a news agency, ripping the covers off books and magazines that didn't sell. I also learned that he had blond hair, hazy blue eyes, and little penchant for exercise.

When I crossed the gap into some very uninsurance questions, she continued her dispassionate answers, pausing only to glance out the window at the crowd.

"I don't think Perry's ever been married," she said, "but I can't be sure. He and I never delved into the past."

I got the impression the only depths Vaughn delved into were those of her pocketbook.

"Did Perry have money?"

"Sometimes. I knew when he was broke, because then I'd see him more often and he'd be more likely to be straight."

"How straight was he this past week?"

"He got in early a couple of nights, and he seemed to have his head screwed on tighter than usual."

"Did he have a usual hangout?"

"Not really, but he gave me a list of places to call, mostly bars, in case I needed him. Want to see it?"

"Sure."

"Follow me."

She led me up to the second floor. The steps, though carpeted, emitted a chorus of creaks, and her swaying gave me a refresher lesson in anatomy. Her shorts allowed me glimpses of a particularly well developed set of muscles high on the outside of her thighs. Phil Fleming, that expert in body-shaping equipment, could probably give the technical name for those muscles, but I wasn't interested. Like the unschooled art lover, I knew what I liked.

At the top of the stairs, I said, "Did you have an accident at work?"

"You saw my bruises?"

I nodded.

"Just some more of Fleming's handiwork. His company's been promising for six months to fix our leg-press machine. Part of it fell on me the other day."

She hiked up one leg of her shorts to reveal a thigh ringed with bruises. No single blow did that to her, and certainly no machine. Another spot, high on the back of her leg, caught my eye. It was the size of a half-dollar.

"Nice tattoo," I said. Sky blue, it was a bird in flight, with details etched in fine black lines.

"Brand-new. I got it as a surprise for Perry. That was his nickname for me. Bluebird."

I followed her into the bedroom. Or, more accurately, the mattress room—because that's what Perry and Michelle slept on. No box springs, just a slab of mattress in the center of the room. Stacks of audio equipment lined one wall. Creased and yellowed posters of rock stars popular five years ago decorated the room.

The closet door was open. Judging from the visible part of Perry's wardrobe, he could have bought several stereos with what he spent on clothing.

A heavy perfume clogged the air, and I took note of specks of glass on the floor by the dresser. Michelle must have missed them when cleaning the room. I wondered if the broken perfume bottles were another ''accident.''

''Here.''

She handed me a sheet of notebook paper. Printed on it were the names of over twenty bars and restaurants. Murray's wasn't listed. Neither was the Fitch.

''Whenever I wanted to contact Perry, I'd start at the top of the list and call my way down.''

''This sounds silly, but was Perry or any of his friends involved in entertainment?''

''Silly, yes. Perry didn't have friends in entertainment because he simply didn't have any *friends.*''

''Except you.''

She didn't answer.

''Did he ever show an interest in magic?''

''He'd sometimes read my *Fate* magazine.''

''Not that kind of magic. *This* kind.''

I took the manicuring scissors off her dresser and cut one of her stereo speaker cords in three places. She called me a name. I ran the pieces through her hand, restoring the wire. She liked the trick, but didn't apologize for the name-calling.

''Must be a fun hobby,'' she said. ''No. He didn't do tricks. You asked that because he died at the Fitch, where all those magicians hang out. Right?''

I nodded and said, ''I heard that Sheriff Tarrant gave him a hard time. Did Perry deserve it?''

''No matter what Perry did, he didn't deserve Tarrant. I don't know what Tarrant did to him each time he rousted him, but Perry would never be the same for days afterward. He'd never talk about it.''

''Can you tell me about Perry's activities the day before yesterday?''

''Not much. He was under the covers when I left for work, and he was gone when I returned.''

''What time?''

''I left before five in the morning. It's a forty-minute drive, and it was my turn to open the spa. We have special sessions for people who want to exercise before going to work. I didn't get back until well after dark. Every Monday I have an evening class for women who work during the day. That's why I was gone so long. My schedule at the club is uneven. Today I don't have to go in at all, yet I'll be there eleven hours tomorrow. When that deputy called last night to tell me about Perry, I was in the middle of preparing this yard sale.''

I asked questions about clowns and makeup but only got puzzled looks. She knew about Vaughn getting trapped in the safe, but not about how he was dressed. I didn't tell her.

There was no need to ask who Vaughn's enemies were. She would have just handed me the Roselle phone book and told me to open to any page.

''Your questions are starting to get queer, mister. Perry's insurance is paid up, I'm the beneficiary, and no one's cheating me out of it.''

''How long have you known each other?''

''A year. His parents took out the insurance for him when he was a kid. They were the original beneficiaries, but they've been dead for years. Perry recently dug out the policy and wondered if it was worth anything. He called a salesman from your company, but all the guy wanted was to sell him more insurance. Perry said that he didn't need more, that the only people who needed insurance were those who crossed his path. Finally, the salesman advised Perry to change the beneficiary. So he named me. It's the only gift he ever gave me, so I didn't argue.''

Her eyes were dry. She didn't sniffle. I was more grieved when my ant farm froze in the third grade.

I didn't ask about the face value of the policy. That might have exposed me. Since she seemed more curious than greedy about the insurance, it was probably no more than several thousand.

''You're probably wondering what I saw in him,'' she said. ''Well, Perry took care of me. He protected me. When people learned that I was his girl, they never hassled me. Creeps knew better than to flirt with me.''

I wondered what happened when *she* initiated the flirting. How did he protect her then? Were her bruises and broken perfume bottles examples of his protection?

A picture taped to the wall among the posters caught my attention. Done with colored felt-tip pens, it reminded me of the cover of a fantasy magazine. It showed a man astride a motorcycle as big as a bulldozer. Fair-skinned with beacon-like eyes, he was an unwilling passenger rather than a rider. He wore a silver Nazi helmet and had blond, shoulder-length hair. A biker Viking.

''You're talented,'' I said.

''No. Perry drew that.''

''Did he do others?''

''Loads. He'd draw when he was bored. I threw out all his pictures this morning. I guess I forgot that one. All unsalable items got Glad-Bagged.''

''A pity. Does that guy in the picture look anything like Perry?''

''No. Perry was more muscular, but not that good-looking. He never drew anything of himself. He loved to draw bikes and planes and guns. He always waited until he was almost finished before he put any people in his pictures. He said they were the hardest to do.''

''You don't have a photo of him?''

She shook her head.

I said, ''One more question: why did he go to the Fitch the other night?''

''To rip it off.''

''He told you?''

''No. Sheriff Tarrant did.''

I could have told her that even if the life insurance was in force, death in the commission of a felony would void the policy. I decided to let the real insurance man do that job.

I again looked over the list she had given me. Out of the corner of my eye, I saw her fluff up the pillows and ease herself down on the mattress. She raised her T-shirt until it was even with the bottom of her breasts, then slid her fingers a few inches inside the waistband of her shorts. I pretended not to notice, bringing the list closer and turning away from her.

Squabbling voices peppered with profanity rose from the crowd outside. It drew us both to the window. Her shirt rose even higher, giving me a long look at what I had passed up. Outside, two women were playing tug-of-war with a leather motorcycle jacket. Perry's.

She sighed and said, "I'd better go down and referee the vultures." With reluctance, she lowered her T-shirt, tugging until its lettering was again readable.

"One more thing. Are you taking care of the funeral arrangements?"

"I'm paying for it, but there won't be much. He's already been cremated. The ceremony will be brief."

"Cremated? That's what he wanted?"

"More or less. He once told me what kind of funeral he'd like, but we couldn't carry out all his wishes completely."

"Why not?"

"He wanted the cremation to take place on the abandoned railroad tracks, in the middle of the garbage."

I lingered at the window, staring beyond the arguing women at a man slowly going through a box of record albums as though the heavy-metal rock were made of gold.

Jeffers.

I blamed luck for bringing him here, but knew it was anything but.

"Could I use your phone?"

"Help yourself."

I followed her down to the living room, where I flipped through her phone book. I closed it after she went out to supervise the sale. Her phone rang. I answered it.

"Blue's? NcNair Travel here to confirm you for the 902 at six P.M. on Thursday."

"Refresh my memory, please. The destination of the 902?" I said.

"Fort Lauderdale."

"One-way?"

"Yes."

"Double fare?"

"No. Single. If you want to change that, we'll—" I hung up.

I saw Michelle's purse on the couch. A book of matches stuck out of it. Unusual for an exercise instructor. I took the matches out and read the cover. Either she was having an affair with the famous singer, or she had once stayed at a motel called Torme's. I replaced the matches.

I kept watch from the pantry window. It took a full twenty minutes for Jeffers to make his move. While Michelle counted the dollar bills in her cigar box, he walked to the rear of the house. I went out the front. On the porch I passed the teenage boy, returning with his dad to make the big purchase of his life: one used custom Honda with sissy bar, crash bars, and AM-FM cassette, with bad karma thrown in at no extra cost.

CHAPTER TEN

The restaurant's name was Corky's Eating Village, and what an antiquated village it was. The phone booth was made of wood, and it had a sliding glass door that switched on a light when I closed it.

Though Corky's was only ten miles out of town, I had taken an hour to drive to it, wanting to be sure I had shaken Jeffers.

Five people formed a line outside the booth. The guy in front said, "Shake it up, buddy. Buy some gas and go *see* your woman if you love her that much."

When Jack answered the phone, he immediately consented to lend me his Polaroid, and I was glad he didn't ask why I needed it. I asked him to get Cate on the phone, and I waited another three minutes. By now the line outside the booth had grown to seven.

When Cate picked up the phone, she said, "Can you make it short, Harry? Quimp and the others are waiting. And speak up. My clown hat's covering my ears. I don't want to unpin it."

"What's Spillman having you do today?"

"You left before reveille?"

"I missed that treat."

"At six A.M. Quimp woke us up with reveille played on a crank organ. When Rupeka didn't get up right away, Quimp dumped a bucket of ice water on him. He almost slugged Quimp."

"Turned against his mentor, did he? Wish I had seen that."

"We're apple-eating now."

"What's that?"

"Eating fruit in character."

"Yes, I see. Of course. And how, pray tell, does the proper Quimp eat?"

"I can tell you this much: he doesn't talk with his mouth full."

I laughed and said, "I need a favor."

Before I detailed my request, I had to promise to coach her for a solid hour later. I talked loud so she could hear me above the increasingly angry throng waiting for my phone. There was a honking in the background at Cate's end.

"Who's that? Quimp?"

"Yes. After he gave us instructions this morning, he stopped speaking. One honk means yes, and two is no."

I asked if Quimp had intended to be in makeup yesterday, the day we found the body.

"Let me think. Yes, I think he told us he was going to wear makeup for yesterday's evening session."

"Put Quimp on, please."

Cate asked him if he wanted to talk to me, then gave him the phone. Six honks in a row blasted my ear. He was one torqued-off clown.

"Sorry to interrupt, Marcus—I mean Quimp—but I think you should call off your contest."

Honk honk.

"You might have been the target, instead of Vaughn. You and your group could be in danger. You should—"

Honk honk.

"Okay, be that way. Put Cate back on. At least she—"

There was a nonstop spate of honking followed by what sounded like someone hitting the telephone with the horn. He hung up. If he often threw tantrums like that, it would be easy to imagine someone deciding to permanently shut him up with a spin of the combination dial.

The crowd waiting for the phone, now numbering over twenty, had turned ugly. They refused to clear a path when I exited the booth. I flung a ball of flame in the air, and it broke into a shower of sparks. They cowered, shielding their eyes. I walked fast, hoping that none of Corky's Eating Villagers got the notion that my fireball was a work of Satan and that I should be seized, carried to the kitchen, and grilled alive in punishment.

Kenneth Ratcliff looked fit. With animation, he described all his ails.

"The accident happened on the set of *Venus Voodoo*. I never regained full use of my legs and left shoulder. The film studio settled handsomely with me. I invested wisely and have lived off that since the fifties."

Jack O'Connell had already told me Ratcliff's story, but he hadn't specified that once I got off the highway there'd still be a wrenching half hour of unpaved roads before I reached Ratcliff's house. The last leg of the journey shook all the excess rust from my van. Anyone living here would have to be a hermit.

Ratcliff had been a promising young film actor until his mishap. Sitting in his living room, he was now living up to his current billing as a local eccentric. Jack told me that Ratcliff occasionally used his skills to help the local community theatre when they were stuck for special makeup effects.

Movie fan magazines lay all around the room. Framed pictures of stars, all contemporaries of Brando during his torn T-shirt days, hung on the walls. I had heard stories of faded Hollywood luminaries who pined away in loneliness for their glory days, but Ratcliff had never made any movies to be wistful about. *Venus Voodoo* would have been his first. He was nostalgic for days that never were, days that only *could* have been.

He was pushing sixty, but his chiseled face bore hardly any marks of age, as though a sculptor had created it by using as few hammer strikes as possible. The years had affected only Ratcliff's eyesight. He was badly nearsighted.

He poured me a drink from an unlabeled jug from his fridge. It looked and smelled like antifreeze. I wondered if it had been drained from the junked DeSoto up on blocks on his front lawn. I put the glass on the end table and hoped he wouldn't notice my lack of thirst. I listened to his stories.

"Ah. The role of Bob the geologist in *Swamp Woman* could have been mine. Roger Corman himself called and begged me to take the role. You know who got it? A guy by the name of Touch Connors. What a waste. That part was *me*. I lied and told Roger I was feeling well, but he saw through me."

This was his third tale of how fate had cheated him out of movie parts. The movies he regretted missing—*Eegah!*, *Robot Monster*, and *Jet Attack*—were all famous for being extraordinarily awful. With taste that bad, even if Ratcliff had gotten the parts he now mooned over, his career still would have nose-dived.

He started another yarn, but I cut him short. "Mr. Ratcliff, could you make me up like Quimp, that famous clown?"

"What? You back again? I didn't recognize you at first. If you hadn't been so damned impatient the other night, I could have shown you how to apply the makeup yourself. Then you wouldn't have to bug me. Are you willing to pay me the same price? Five hundred?"

"You've got me confused with someone else."

He leaned close and squinted at me, reading me as though I were an item on a bulletin board. "Could have fooled me."

"When did this other person ask you to do the makeup?"

"Day before yesterday. He brought pictures with him."

He waved pages torn from a recent *People* magazine, all color photos of Quimp.

"Can you describe this guy?"

He tried, but ended up rambling about the man's uncanny resemblance to Frank Sinatra, Jr. In a few seconds he changed that to Elisha Cook, Jr.; then Efrem Zimbalist, Jr.; and then Junior Samples.

"Was this man in costume?"

"Yes."

"Gloves and all?"

He nodded.

Before I left, I noticed a new video recorder, store tags still on it, atop his TV. The price tag said five hundred dollars.

Now he could watch over and over all the bad movies that he never got to make.

CHAPTER ELEVEN

Moving day at the Fitch.

Men dollied boxes and furniture onto a moving van, then went back inside for more—worker ants in wool hats and stained sweatshirts.

Inside, Jack stood at the registration desk, watching the procession. His cigar having gone out, he relit it, tilting his head so that the lighter wouldn't burn his nose. "We're dismantling the bar today," he said. "Everything goes but the liquor. That'll become my private stock and should last well into the next century. Spillman and his people can use the barroom now. He told me the conference room was getting cramped."

"Clowns still at it?" I asked.

His hand drifted inside his cardigan to scratch his chest. "They've knocked off for a while, but Rupeka's still back there. Cate's upstairs. She wanted me to call her when you came in. I gave her that camera you asked for."

"Tell her I'll be talking with Rupeka."

The conference room was as cool as the mid-April air outside. It smelled of cold cream and Ben-Gay. Rupeka sat straddling a metal folding chair, flattening his chest against its back. Looking as though he had just run five fast miles, he nodded at me and drank from his bottle of Gatorade. He wore a T-shirt bearing the faded name of his police academy.

"All done?" I said.

"No, just break time. There's another session this evening."

"Spillman upstairs?"

"Yeah, he's meditating now. If you interrupt him again, no telling what he might do."

"God forbid another horn-lashing." I turned down Rupeka's offer of a swig from his bottle. "A retired actor did Vaughn's makeup. Do you think Vaughn intended to do more than burgle?"

"That's not my concern. Talk to Tarrant."

"What if Vaughn intended to harm Quimp, even kill him?"

"Quimp has nothing to worry about. Vaughn's dead."

"What if someone hired Vaughn?"

"Who?"

"Look at how arrogant Spillman sometimes is. He's bound to have crossed someone, maybe even one of the clown contestants. One of *you* could have hired Vaughn."

"If it was one of us, why did Vaughn have to go so far out of town for a paid makeup job?"

"It could have been a precaution to divert suspicion away from your group. How'd you know he went out of town to get made up? And that he'd paid for it?"

"Christ," he said tightening the top of his now empty bottle. He lobbed it into a waste can, and it boomed like an explosion.

He got off the chair and stooped to retrieve his wrist watch from his gym bag. His knuckles turned red, then white as he struggled to buckle the band. As he waved away my offer of assistance, I saw that his watch's face was a cartoon of Quimp.

"Jack told me about that actor, too. I merely guessed that Vaughn paid him. From what I've heard about Vaughn, he had only two persuasive techniques: pay 'em or hit 'em."

I told him about the list of bars and other businesses that Michelle had given me. I said, "I haven't contacted them all yet, but so far no one on the list has any complaint about Vaughn raising hell. Looks like he was running a little protection racket, accepting payments to let them alone. Don't you think?''

"Colderwood, don't worry about us clowns. I'm eminently more qualified than you to protect all of us, including your good friend Cate.''

He stalked away. Pausing at the doorway, he bent to adjust his pants cuff. I wondered if I was supposed to see the dull black metal protruding from worn leather on his ankle—a revolver in an ankle holster.

I gazed out the conference-room window at the excavation crew scooping out a crater two lots down from the Fitch. Cate walked into the room, and I didn't recognize her at first because she was still in full costume and makeup. On a subconscious level she had absorbed Quimp's mannerisms—his dainty walk and waddling torso. She held a sheet of paper in one hand and a munched-on fish sandwich in the other. Dangling on her arm was a tote bag full of gag props. The head of a rubber chicken and a giant kitchen match stuck out at the top.

I told her about Michelle Blue and Kenneth Ratcliff while she sat on a folding chair and made checks on her paper. She nibbled on her sandwich, which looked cold. I saw what was on the paper, and was amazed at how much she had done.

"I'm making sure I didn't skip anyone," she said. "These three are the ones I couldn't pin down."

There were twenty-three names on her list—all the people who registered at the Fitch in the last week but weren't part of the Magicade Convention. She had circled the names Ralph Kendall, Dwight May, and James Loy.

"New Jersey directory assistance has numbers for Kendall and May, but neither answered his phone. There is no James Loy listed for any address in Battle Creek, Michigan. I called the Chamber of Commerce, and they're checking Loy's address to see if it's a fake. We didn't have as many calls as you thought, because most of the people

at the Fitch the last few days were conventioneers. In addition to giving me the guest list, Jack also lent me this.''
She opened her bag to show me the Polaroid. "I made some calls on lunch break, and Jack did the rest.''

"Great. But if this Loy guy turns out to be legit, we'll have to tackle the list of conventioneers. Did you get the, uh . . . ?''

She nodded, and rummaged through her bag. She pulled out the rubber chicken and a whipped-cream can and dropped them carelessly on the floor. When she removed the two-foot-long match, she accidentally brushed its head against the edge of the bag. A tiny door at the top of the match popped open and a cuckoo sprang out, holding a burning, normal-size match in its beak. She blew out the flame and set it aside.

"Ah, here." She removed a jumbo can of hard candy. The oldest and most popular practical joke in the book: open the can, and four spring snakes explode from it.

She offered me the can, and I said, "No. *You.*"

She unscrewed the cap, and a lone snake flew out and bounced off the ceiling. She dipped her hand into the can and pulled out a revolver. She held it on her finger by the trigger guard.

"Smith & Wesson .44 Special. Good. Same as Tarrant's,'' I said. "When did you get time to go to a gun shop? I thought there was a waiting period for these.''

"Does it look new to you?''

It didn't. Maybe not as worn as Rupeka's piece, but definitely not new.

"Who—?''

"Jack loaned it to us. He still has a mini-arsenal from the days when he was what he calls a professional paranoic.''

Remembering the gun barrel I faced when Jack opened the safe, I thought that maybe his paranoia wasn't over yet.

"You told him why we need it?''

"Yes. He approves, but wishes the circumstances were different.''

I made sure the pistol was empty, then stuffed it into my coat pocket. I put the spring snake back into the can, sticking it in my other pocket.

"By the way, I think Quimp noticed the improvements in my Peekaboo Entrance."

"Great. What else did you do today?"

"So far: elementary juggling, two sessions of meditation while staring at eight-by-ten glossies of Quimp, and calisthenics. Hodge, the magic collector, was the only one that couldn't keep up with the exercises. Novak really surprised me. I think he's in better shape than Rupeka. And, oh yes. I forgot. We did blocks, too."

"Blocks?"

"For an hour we played with plastic snap-together blocks. No explanation why. I suppose that's no weirder than some of the acting-class drills I've done."

"Rupeka said there'll be a night session. Why?"

"Who knows? Today a department store delivered luminous safety vests. We must be going outside. What are you planning?"

"First I'm going to find a safe place for this six-shooter. Then I'm going to—oh hell."

"What's wrong?"

"Everything."

Through the conference-room and office doors, I could see Jeffers standing at the registration desk, gawking as if he were killing time on a street corner.

I flattened against the wall.

"Who's he?" Cate asked.

"His name's Jeffers. We're playing a game, and he wants to make me the big loser."

"Can I help?"

"Get the door."

She put both hands on the door and pushed it away from her gently but firmly, as though it were an unwelcome suitor at a dance. I barely heard it click shut. I sized up the window and knew it would be a tight squeeze. I took offense when she named which parts of my body could benefit from her husband's equipment—even though I was thinking the same thing.

I opened the window, and the grind and drone of excavation machinery poured in. At the base of the sill there were scrape marks from when Vaughn supposedly had pried his way in. I put the camera strap around my neck and hoisted myself up until my waist was level with the sill. Halfway out, I saw how far it was to the ground. I momentarily froze, but resumed my wriggling in a few seconds and realized I was stuck. The window frame firmly entrapped the very same spongy parts of my anatomy that Cate had ridiculed.

Someone knocked on the conference-room door.

"Don't answer yet," I said. The roar of the earth scoopers made it hard to hear my own voice.

I thought I heard Cate say, "One moment."

She tried to push me through the window, and I took perverse pleasure in the pressure of her hands. The gun in my pocket dug into my hip. The hard candy can in the other didn't help matters.

"Push Harry, push," she said.

I tried to come back into the room, but still couldn't budge. A man wearing a hard hat walked over to underneath the window and said, "Come on, buddy, you can do it. I skipped many a room bill myself. Keep wiggling." His words were unclear because his lip was fat with a healthy dip of snuff.

I heard the scratch followed by the cuckoo's call. I screamed even before the flame burned me. "Cate put away that damned match!"

What else did she have in her bag of clown tricks? Maybe the . . .

She had already gotten the idea. There was a hiss. The coolness soothed my burn, and I smelled the sweetness of the whipped cream. Would it be enough lubrication to get me free?

Cate took a running start and rammed me. I went out the window like a pilot ejecting with no parachute from a doomed plane. Luckily the man below kept his hard hat on. Otherwise I'd have mussed his hair when I landed on his head. His hat nearly broke my ribs.

After we got to our feet, he adjusted his hat and said (I translate from the language of snuffese): "Follow me."

I did.

We jogged across a no-man's-land of crusted dirt. Side-stepping mud craters, we ducked behind a dump truck. I leaned against the truck and caught my breath while he did a victory whoop.

I asked for and he cheerfully gave me his hard hat, safety glasses, and even the round leather holster that held his snuff can. He looked offended when I offered him money. When I asked to borrow the truck, he stopped looking offended and held out his hand. Our deal depleted all my pocket cash. He didn't question why a man with cash would be dodging a hotel bill.

As I pulled myself into the truck cab, he said with embarrassment, "Buddy, there's whipped cream on your ass. You'll get it all over the seat." He lent me a red hanky with white posies, and I cleaned it off. "That must be one hell of a party you're running from."

After giving me a quick driving lesson, he got out. I didn't think he was authorized to lend me the truck because he made me promise to forget I had ever seen him. What I did forget was how to get the truck out of the lower two gears. I didn't care. Once I got this hulk rolling, who was going to stop me?

I eased it out into the street and chugged past the Fitch at seven-miles-per. Jeffers was on the sidewalk in front of the awning. He looked up and down the street while Cate tried to block his view by waving clown props and doing shtick. I gave a long blast on the horn and looked back at them through the side mirror. That's why I didn't see my van in time to avoid sideswiping it. There was a long squeal, followed by a scraping sound. I hoped damage was minimal and vowed to learn to stop the truck before I demolished something not on the wreckers' schedule.

I double-parked two blocks from the hotel, leaving the keys in the ignition and my worker's disguise on the seat. When I slammed the door, I still felt in character, as if I had just put in a tough ten hours of digging and wrecking and that a beer along with the *Six O'Clock News* would be a great way to top off the day. I turned away from the truck and walked smack into Jeffers.

His late-model Chevy, chromeless and khaki-colored (perfect urban camouflage), was triple-parked beside the truck. He had left his engine running and driver's door open.

It was unmistakably Jeffers. His doll's nose and close-set eyes had lost none of their charm. He had eyes that always said, "Trust me." I had. Once. Never again.

The last time I saw Jeffers this close had been a year ago, almost to the day, in Oklahoma. He always intentionally dressed to blend into the locale. That year, in his felt Stetson and fresh denim, he looked the part of a dude. Today he sported a light blue spring suit that had probably been on the rack five hours ago. He now wore his hair short and flat, with most of the wave styled out. There was something different about the way he stood. I realized that his wing tips had been altered by the Otis Elevator Company. My theory was that Jeffers had chosen his line of work because of childhood taunts about his height.

He smiled in smug jubilation. When he dipped into his breast pocket, I went for my coat pocket and felt the sleek cold of the pistol.

I admit I briefly considered using it, but I reached in the other pocket and took out the candy can. He unconsciously licked his lips at the sight of the treat. I opened the lid and snaked his face. He beat the air with his hands like a man with the DT's.

I hopped in and drove away . . . in his car. He didn't try pursuing me in the dump truck.

I drove around Roselle for an hour, taking in the sights and looking out for Jeffers. I parked his car in a safe neighborhood and walked the six blocks to the hotel. As I passed my van, I assessed its damage. Ugly, but mild. The nasty sanding I had given it revealed lettering that had been painted over. One of the van's previous owners was a diaper service.

I entered the Fitch through the locked service entrance. I could have shouldered the door open, but I didn't have the energy; and I still had my pride. My picking tools did their stuff.

Upstairs, before entering my room, I put my ear to the door, listening for stirring.

All quiet.

Tomorrow I'd ask Jack for another room, even if it was devoid of furniture. Sleeping on the floor would be better than lying awake waiting for Jeffers.

I opened the door.

Sheriff Tarrant sat on my bed. His gun lay beside him. I resisted the impulse to pull out my own gun and ask if he could spare me some bullets. Instead, I grasped the Polaroid that was hanging from my neck, aimed it, and snapped his picture.

He extended his hand, indicating he wanted to shake mine. When I reached for it, he dipped down quick and pulled the carpet out from under me. I went down, hitting the back of my head on the bottom of the door. I hugged the camera to my chest. Miniature Tarrants kaleidoscoped around me. They were all laughing.

CHAPTER TWELVE

Every time my heart beat, my head hurt, so I tried stopping my heart. When that failed, I struggled to a sitting position and waited for everything in the room to stop circling.

Tarrant played the patience game, too, studying me for further signs of recovery. I tried for a dull expression, the kind that used to persuade teachers not to call on me. Deciding I wasn't entertainment enough, Tarrant clicked on the TV. Bedsprings squeaked as he got up, worsening my head's pounding.

While he adjusted the picture, I rubbed my skull and found no bumps. He turned his attention back to me. My eyes must have lost some of their glassiness, because he broke his silence. I noticed that Tarrant wore a Band-Aid above one eye. The flesh surrounding it was inflamed.

"You're probably wondering what happened to my eye," he said. "I arrested a burglar yesterday. Real odd duck. Wouldn't listen to reason. Don't feel sorry for me. He looks a lot worse. You know, Jack O'Connell's an odd duck, too. This place'll be rubble soon, yet he still shampoos the rugs. I forgot to warn you. It was still wet. Very slippy."

He picked up his gun by the barrel and swung it close to my face. I shrank back, not wanting a steady diet of Excedrin for the next month.

I felt the pressure of my pistol in my pocket, and I hoped he wouldn't frisk me. If his finger ventured near the trigger of his gun, I'd use mine. He pulled the gun away from my face and turned back to the snowy television.

"Jeez, ever see a hotel TV with a decent picture? Even the sound's bad."

He jammed his gun butt through the screen and jumped back. It went poof, and the sound died. After the smoke cleared, he put his gun on the dresser and picked up the TV, dragging the plug from the wall.

"Always wanted to do this when I was a kid. How about you?"

He walked to the window and tried to raise it while still maintaining a grip on the television. When the window wouldn't budge, he heaved the TV like a medicine ball through the glass. It crashed to the sidewalk, sounding like an auto accident.

"That'll give you the fresh air you need before your trip."

I surveyed the room for a place to dump the pistol. "I'm going nowhere."

Doors slammed in the hall. Windows raised and scared voices wondered what the racket was. In a minute they'd be at my door to check on me.

Tarrant pointed to my overnight bag on the bed. "The problem with travel is that you always buy too many souvenirs. When you try packing, you can't get them all in."

He opened a dresser drawer. "See? You'll never get all this stuff into this measly bag. I'll help." He grabbed handfuls of clothing and tossed them out the window. He did the same with the other drawers.

He unzipped my bag. "See? Crammed with souvenirs."

He turned it upside down and shook it. A spiral notebook fell out. Nothing else. "See? Something like this takes up too much room."

Tarrant thumbed through my book, pausing at some of my entries. He said, "I've always been a big one on taking notes, too. Now here's a good one: *check if T's told truth about V's past—what's T's record as officer?* Gosh, what's

T and V mean? I never was much for codes, but I get the feeling you're learning a lot during your stay in Roselle.''

"I'm learning a lot right now. Why don't you add to my knowledge by telling me when was the last time you saw Vaughn—or should I say V?—alive?''

He grinned, enjoying my transparent attempt to turn the tables. He said, "Glad to oblige. I haven't seen Vaughn for at least a couple of weeks. He had been lying low lately. I think he was using the time to plan this job at the hotel.''

He put the notebook in his pocket and tossed my bag out the window. "Now that you're packed, let's go.''

Where? To his office or out the window?

"There's a trick you used to do on TV," he said. "Confounded the hell out of me. I must have seen it five times. Watch.''

He took an orange silk handkerchief from his pocket and stuffed it into his closed hand. He opened his hand, and the hanky had turned into an egg.

"Hah. Look at me. I'm a magician. You know, the Missis hates magic, but I love it. I figured out how to do this much. Show me the rest.''

That did it. Break into my room. Read my secret diary. Assault me. Hold me prisoner. But don't screw with my magic.

"Be careful," I said. "That's a handmade egg.''

"You're telling me. A foot away, I can't tell it from the real thing.''

"It was a gift. Harry Kellar was its original owner.''

"Never heard of him. Just show me the rest. How do you turn it into a real egg?'' He deliberately dropped it on the floor, and it smashed, revealing the handkerchief hidden inside.

Someone knocked at the door. "Hey. You okay in there?'' It was Lorenz Novak.

Fighting dizziness, I held on to the doorknob and pulled myself to my feet. I staggered into Tarrant's arms. He brushed me away, and I grabbed the dresser to keep from falling back down.

"Better tell your concerned friend you're okay."

I raised my voice. "I'm all right, Novak. I tried to open the window, and the damn thing fell apart on me."

"He's okay," Novak said to the others in the hall.

The sheriff smiled with approval. I ran my fingers over the metal hidden behind my back. Step one complete.

I took time to adjust the ratchets. Everything had to be just right. For onstage stunts, I was always in complete control; but for this, the best I could do was try to relax. And hope. The rings and chain concealed behind me put me on familiar turf, and my confidence grew.

I reeled and stumbled into him again. His eyes snapped wary as he realized something was afoot. Or should I say a-wrist? I executed steps two through six of my routine without a hitch.

Before moving back to view my handiwork, I invented a step seven: I stole his gun.

All I wanted now was out. Fast. I felt like a cowboy escaping from the corral after enraging the bull.

But when I got to the door, I stopped to gloat.

The sheriff lunged for me, but the bed I had handcuffed him to jerked him back. With his handcuff key in my pocket, I felt on top of the world. I emptied the bullets from his gun and pitched them out the window.

Using my own regulation cuffs, I often performed this same stunt in my act. The real trick with Tarrant had been to lift his cuffs and keys without his knowing.

I said, "You asked about stuff I did as a kid. Funny thing. The neighborhood kids were afraid to play with me. Take hide-and-seek, for example. When I played, weird stuff always happened to the guy who was It."

Tarrant reddened. He struggled, but moved the bed only an inch. My phone rang, and I picked it up.

"Hello." The long-distance connection sounded like running water.

"Harry?" It was Stanley Trimble.

"How's Allentown?" I asked.

"Peachy. What kind of hotel is that Fitch? I tried to get through eight times. One time I got a honking horn."

"Oh, the Fitch is undergoing changes, the most drastic of which will occur in two or three days. Even my room has been redecorated since I arrived. They've recently air-conditioned it and sent my TV out for repairs."

"Swell. When can I expect you?"

"I'll call before I leave."

I held the receiver away from me as Trimble threatened me with everything from lawsuits to violence. I put the phone back to my ear. Trimble was saying," . . . and I got to worrying that you were in Dutch, so I called the law. Guess what the sheriff there said? He begged me to get you out of his hair. He says that if you don't lay off, you'll get a striped suntan from the sun shining through the bars of his lockup. Come to Allentown, Harry. I just signed you with a great company. Did you ever hear stories of how some stupid people have bathed their dogs and actually tried to dry them in microwave ovens, only to have the dogs explode? Well, the MicroDog Corporation has a device that allows you to microwave dogs dry *safely*. I bet there's a slew of tricks you could invent to . . ."

I gave the phone to Tarrant so he could listen to the latest in explosion-free pet care. He tossed it on the floor and reached with his free hand into his pocket. Of course, his key was gone, but he did find the egg I planted there, the real one I normally used in the handkerchief-to-egg trick. He withdrew a gooey hand.

"Hide your eyes and count to one hundred, Sheriff. By *ones*, not tens. I must inform you that the hard part about playing hide-and-seek with me is that I don't tell you where home base is. No peeking, now."

Out in the hall, I slammed the door and pretended to be winded. Standing in front of me were Spillman, Cate, and Novak. Cate had a what-the-hell-are-you-up-to look. I gave Tarrant's gun to Novak. He held it as though it were a poisonous snake.

"Prowler. In my room," I said, wedging words in between breaths. "Handcuffed to my bed. Don't go in. Might still be dangerous. I'm okay; but he busted things up pretty good. I'll call the sheriff. Don't go in till Tarrant shows up."

Once I was on my way down the steps, I slowed down. I estimated I had thirty minutes to get my van off the street and find another place to stay. Then I'd have all night to consider whether staying here was worth it anymore.

CHAPTER THIRTEEN

The street lamp in front of the hotel cast an exaggerated shadow of my every move. Looking up, I found it easy to pick out my room. Its window frame glinted with jagged glass. I gathered up my belongings from the street and sidewalk. One pair of socks lay atop the smashed television.

I retreated up the block to my van, where I stowed my stuff. I then cruised nearby streets, searching for a hiding place for my vehicle.

I parked in the middle of a row of vans, trucks, and RVs, under a banner that said, "JEB'S CREAMPUFF CITY." It reminded me of Ben's Motormart in Georgia, where I'd originally bought my van. I knew I'd have to return early tomorrow, before Jeb and his crew got their mitts on my van—before they rolled back the mileage, pounded out the dents, repainted it, and shipped it out of state. Possibly back to Ben's Motormart where, if I wanted it back badly enough, I could get swindled all over again.

Wearing a silvery robe, Cate sat at her dresser-desk. A pair of small-lensed reading glasses lay atop two bound stacks of paper. I admired her ability to concentrate in spite of the evening's disturbances. As I had never seen her wear glasses, I tried to visualize their effect. I wasn't sure I liked the image.

Cate raised her voice to be heard over the pounding in

the next room. Jack and Rupeka were nailing boards over the window that Tarrant had broken.

"By the time the deputy showed up," she was saying, "Jack had already hacksawed off the cuffs. The sheriff had calmed down to the point where he no longer mentioned your name and lynch mobs in the same sentence."

"You're sure I'm not a fugitive?"

"Officially, you aren't. Tarrant told Deputy Wirfel that he'd bring no charges against you. He would consider it a prank. He said arresting you would be more trouble than it's worth, but I think he knew he'd look foolish in court. You completely disarmed him using misdirection. I'd still stay out of his way."

"What did Jack say about the damage?"

"The sheriff offered restitution, along with embarrassed apologies, but Jack refused, saying the TV was worthless and that the sheriff had only started something the wrecking crews would finish in a few days."

"I'll lay low for a while. I'll use the back entrance, and I'll ask Jack for another room, unless you're willing to—"

She smiled and said, "Sorry. Too crowded here already. Are you also switching rooms because of that little guy who chased you today?"

"That little guy's name is Jeffers, and I'd prefer not to talk about him. No use making a lousy day lousier."

She frowned, letting the matter pass. "There are still more names from the registration book to run down, but that James Loy seems to be a ghost. The name is phony, and there's no such number or address in Battle Creek."

"Does Jack remember him?"

"Nope. The convention demanded all Jack's attention. According to the guest book, Loy checked in the day before the convention and checked out closing day."

"During tonight's session with the clowns, how about asking if any of them know Loy?"

"Tonight's session is canceled. We won't meet until tomorrow morning. After the commotion, Spillman—"

"Don't tell me. He thought the vibes weren't right."

"Something like that. Where you going now?"

I realized that I had been fidgeting and glancing at the door. "When I was outside, I saw a light on in the basement. I'm going down to check on it."

"That's Hodge."

"He must be sifting through the magic collection in the basement, right? He probably didn't hear the racket. Is Rupeka with him?"

"No, Rupeka said he was going out for a bite to eat. Harry, there's something screwy about Rupeka I can't put my finger on."

"He does seem overly tense."

She put on her glasses. I was wrong. They added intrigue, not plainness. She opened one of the binders on the desk. "Movie or play?" I asked.

"This one's a proposed made-for-TV science fiction movie."

"Lead role?"

"No, it's not right for me, but the villainess suits me fine. The other one's a stage play."

I interpreted "not right" as "too young," and I wondered if she still blamed me for her stalled acting career.

She found the creased page that marked her place. I remembered her always studying manuscripts backstage before we went on. Back in our motel room, she often got me to read the other parts. There were a few times she actually had a script in her hands just minutes after we had made love.

And phones. She treated them as mystic oracles. *"Don't talk long. That producer might try to get through."* I grew to hate it when the phone rang, because I too felt acute disappointment if the caller had bad news.

She got a disgusted look, flopped the script closed, and opened the other one—the play. I could see the *Variety* headline: "Cate Fleming Leaves TV Movies for Broadway." My own humor didn't amuse me.

I gently placed both hands on her shoulders until she turned toward me, and I kissed her. She didn't seem to enjoy it, nor did she seem to mind. She removed her glasses, lightly circled her fingers behind my neck, and returned the kiss. It wasn't at all like the one I'd just given her, nor like any I remembered from years before. There was timidity, guilt, and distaste in it. It was the kiss of a—

"—married woman. I'm a married woman now, Harry," she said.

"We're all married to something."

"No. *You're* married to something. I'm married to *somebody,* and I'm going to see it through. Good or bad."

She pulled the loosened halves of her robe close together. I looked down at her script, hoping what she just said was a line stolen from the playwright.

"Can I leave my overnight bag here?" Before she could protest, I added, "Only until I get another room."

"Where are you going now?"

"I won't be back until tomorrow morning. I'm taking a trip thirty years into the future."

I thought of Hodge in the basement and said, "First I'll take a journey into the past—" I remembered her kiss. "Again."

She returned to her playscript. Funny how reading made her blink so much. Must be the glasses.

Jack, hammer in hand and apron of nails around his waist, met me in the hall. "We're a full-service hotel," he said. "You want food? Just call us. You want laundry? Call us. You bust up your room to smithereens? Just call, and we'll slap things together again. You and Tarrant should start a rock band. You two already got hotel-wrecking down cold."

Novak came out of my room, sucking his thumb. "My apprentice," Jack said.

"You're supposed to hit *your* thumb, not mine," Novak said.

"You want me to kiss it so it feels better? Oh, I forgot. That's not a sophisticated enough method for you. You'd like to put on a beanie, hide in your room, and *think* away the black-and-blue.''

Novak forced an ice smile and displayed his bruised thumb. ''He scoffs at my theories, but I'll bet you two hundred dollars that by tomorrow you won't be able to tell one thumb from the other.''

''Want to see me make one just like the other right now? It'll take two seconds,'' Jack said, waving his hammer.

Novak stuck his thumb in front of my face. ''Mr. Colderwood? Care to wager against my ability to accelerate the healing process?''

''Yeah, Harry,'' Jack said. ''Didn't you used to offer a reward to anyone who could do the supernatural?''

''I offered ten thousand dollars to anyone who, under scientific conditions, could perform a paranormal feat.''

''You never lost the money?'' Novak asked.

''Never came close, although many tried for it. I was glad my offer got plenty of publicity, because it brought more careful public scrutiny of wild claims by so-called psychics. The press has a funny habit of dissecting a politician's tax returns, but further down the same page, uncritically reporting a crackpot's claims of mental key-bending, haunted houses, or extraterrestrial visitors. Today my disbelief in matters psychic is stronger than ever. To answer your next question: yes, the money is all gone. I used it a long time ago. I couldn't perform the supernatural, either—I couldn't live without eating.

''Although I do accept the idea that emotions play a significant role in the body's healing processes, I wonder if your claims don't veer too far from accepted medical findings. I must read your next book.''

''That won't be for a while. I'm taking a break from writing because I recently lost an entire manuscript. After this clown competition's over, I'll be starting over again. I'll give you one of my previous books.''

''No thanks. I'll buy it.''

''Want to be totally objective, eh?''

''Don't you?''

"I just came from your hotel room where it's evident that *someone* lost his objectivity. You may think this pompous, but maybe yesterday could have been avoided if Perry Vaughn had read one of my books."

"What do you mean?"

"Vaughn smothered. Had he read *Mind Relax,* he could have slowed down his metabolism and survived long enough to be rescued."

I said, "Sure, and if you toss how-to-swim manuals into a pool of drowning people, maybe one of them will read fast enough to learn the Australian crawl. I'm not saying relaxation doesn't affect bodily functions. I do question whether you can apply it in a panic situation like being locked in an airtight metal box." I didn't add that I had tried and failed.

He said, "I thought I'd feel at home with magicians, but these past few days I've been treated with coldness and rudeness."

"No, you're at home, all right. You and I are both entertainers who fool people. The only difference with you is that you won't admit it."

"Read my books before you jump to conclusions," Novak said. He went off to his room, thumb in mouth.

"No sense of humor," Jack said.

"Oh, he's got a sense of humor," I insisted. "Just no timing."

Laughter, all canned, billowed from Novak's room. The floor and walls vibrated with Bill Cosby's childhood memories, full volume.

"Jack." I talked so low he had to step closer to hear. "I hope you didn't work too hard in there."

"Nah, just wanted to keep the cold air out these last few days. I've been thinking of turning off the heat the last day the clowns are here, and maybe setting up some space heaters in the lobby."

"Not a bad idea. By the way, I won't be using this room anymore."

He winked and said, "Cate's?"

"No, a different room. On another floor."

"There aren't any more beds. We'll move the one from here upstairs tomorrow."

"Don't bother. In my van I have a sleeping bag I use when I can't find lodging."

"There's a nice suite two floors up. I'll get the key."

"Please don't. It's important that no one knows which room I'm in. Including you."

He frowned but knew there was no way to stop my fingers and a few simple tools from opening more doors than all his master keys.

"I need a favor, Jack. It'll be time-consuming, but Cate might help."

"What do you need?"

"Could you check the unoccupied rooms?"

"All of them?"

I nodded.

"What for?"

"I can't say yet, but let me know if you find anything unusual. I suggest you start on the top floor. Also, thanks for lending me the gun. I *will* use it. Cate said you've got a collection?"

"A small one."

"Better take along a pistol on your search. There shouldn't be danger, but just in case."

"How do I contact you when I've completed this waste of time?"

"You can't. I'll be out all night. Just give me the results tomorrow morning."

"Not fair," he said as I started for the stairs. "You carouse all night while I do all the work."

"I'm a magician. I only pretend to carouse, Jack."

An accurate description of what I planned to do.

Hodge was typing while watching TV. At least, that's what it looked like at first.

Sitting in front of a portable computer, he rattled the keyboard with his fingers. Phosphorescent letters appeared, edged their way up the video monitor, and disappeared at the top.

The basement storage room was divided into narrow aisleways of shelves filled with magic relics and memorabilia, the "pieces" donated by magician guests. Hodge's sports coat hung on the back of his chair. His shirt collar was unbuttoned, and he was using his bow tie as a paperweight. A noisy desk fan swiveled back and forth two feet from his face. The room's humidity wilted me in seconds.

"I'm cataloguing the pieces," he said before I could ask. He leaned back in his chair, seeming to welcome the break. The closeness would soon force me topside for fresh air, yet he looked cool and dry.

"I'm curious about what you're doing. I guess everyone asks you the same questions."

"Yep. Everybody. Including Novak. You wouldn't think a guy like that would be interested in magic history."

"You doing this all on your own?"

"Jack's sending this stuff to the American Museum of Magic in Michigan. I'm doing preliminary cataloguing to help the museum get a head start, for no other reason than I love doing it. Jack doesn't know what all's down here. You'd think moisture would have damaged it, but most of it's in good condition."

"How'd you learn about computers?"

He said, "I mostly taught myself, out of necessity. Amazing how much time you save with one of these."

"Aren't you afraid of losing some of your work electronically? I've heard some horror stories about computers."

"It happens, but a friend of mine who's a wiz with computers installed a special circuit he invented that's supposed to cut down on loss from stupid mistakes. In case there's a power failure or I accidentally turn the system off, I can retrieve a limited amount of data that was stored in the computer's memory."

He let me look at the item he was currently working

on—a letter from Houdini to a New York magic dealer, ordering a special latch for one of his escapes.

"Of course, Houdini didn't actually leave this letter here. It was donated by a generous Houdiniana collector."

"You going to finish before these walls come tumbling down?"

"No way," he said. "I'm just getting a feel for what's here. My work will also help alert the shippers which fragile items to take special precautions with."

"Will Jack sell any of this?"

"No. I offered him loads, but he won't hear it."

He invited me to browse, and I made myself at home, soon forgetting the heat. I spent twenty minutes trying to figure out the workings of a banana-colored production box decorated with detailed dragon paintings. Amused at my failure, Hodge punched a few letters and numbers on his keyboard. The computer showed its exquisite manners by flashing an on-screen request that we wait a moment.

Disk drives whistled and clunked. Columns of figures and letters filled the screen. Like magic. Hodge peered at them, as if crystal-gazing, and tapped a finger on one of the lines.

"That piece was donated by Halston Thomas, a magic-shop owner from Bakersfield, California. He had a reputation for craftsmanship and flawless artwork, even though from ten feet away audiences can't distinguish between first- and third-rate quality. He quit his business in the early sixties to fulfill his dream of being a full-time magician."

"The computer told you all that?"

"No, only his name, but I know his work."

"I've never heard of him. Is he still performing?"

"He was a craftsman, not a magician."

"He starved?"

Hodge nodded. "Lasted a year and went back to magic-box making."

"Can your smart machine tell me how this trick works?"

He put his finger on another number on the screen and

dug through a cardboard box full of file folders, extracting the instruction sheet for The Great Halsto's Mystic Box.

Directions at my side, I went step by step through the handling of the trick. When finished, I said, "If his magic performances were as uncreative as this trick, I can see why he went down the tubes." All the box could do was magically produce three silk handkerchiefs, a feat most self-respecting magicians can do barehanded, without all the hardware.

Hodge said, "Those sure are pretty dragons though, aren't they?"

We both smiled knowingly. Amateur magicians around the world had closets and dens crowded with props like this box—beautiful but impractical. Many went unused. Of those who called themselves magicians, only a small percentage actually did shows for pay. Of those, only a fraction made a living at it.

At one time I would have been on such a list. What would the computer say if Hodge entered my name into it? I didn't want to find out, so I put The Great Halsto's Wiz Box back on the shelf, its ineptness no longer amusing me.

Most of the pictures and posters were packed away in boxes, but a few framed photos decorated the walls of the basement room. There was Kalanag floating a woman far over his head and Dante producing a lady assistant from a huge top hat. In another, Dunninger glared at a sealed box with enough severity to burn holes in it.

Not all the pictures were of magicians. I found one that featured a group of men dressed in white robes, but minus the famous hooded masks. Wizards of a different sort.

"The Klan? At the Fitch?" I said.

"Right. There was a rally here back in the twenties. The Fitch wasn't always a magic mecca. Before Jack owned the place, it catered to all sorts. For a while during the fifties, it was a popular stop for traveling sideshows and tent revivalists. Even faith healers."

"Fascinating. You know, bogus faith healers sometimes borrow from the art of magic. I once saw a film on one of those so-called psychic surgeons from the Philippines. He pretended to extract tumors without cutting the skin with a scalpel. He was really using a simple sleight, and the 'tumor' was a raw chicken part.''

In the corner was a metal cabinet with drawers too shallow for file folders. "What's in here?" I asked.

"Films and videotapes. Some are actual records of acts from fifty years ago. Others were recorded right here at the various Magicades.''

I opened a drawer and found rows of labeled metal and plastic containers.

One 16-millimeter film canister was marked "Specialty Acts." It listed performances by Frakson, who worked with cigarettes; Cardini, who did an elegant routine in tails with just cards, cigarettes, and billiards; and (my hero) Think-A-Drink Hoffman.

I walked back to Hodge. When he saw my armload of tapes and films, he removed the diskettes from his computer, filed them in their envelopes, and turned the machine off.

He rubbed his cheeks with his palms and tilted his eyes upward, revealing whites now a filmy red. He scanned the titles I had selected.

"There are two video recorders, a portable TV, and a film projector in that cupboard over there," he said.

"Didn't your mom ever tell you that watching too many movies can ruin your eyes?"

"Sure. Dad used to warn me that magic was the work of the devil, too.''

He connected the VCR while I threaded the projector, following directions inside the machine's cover. For a screen, I plucked a thirty-six-inch white silk handkerchief from Halsto's Whiz Box and tacked it to the wall.

The first reel was a silent performance by Clyde Bradford, filmed at a Boston nightclub in the late thirties. Comedy drunk acts used to be an entertainment staple, and Bradford was one of the best. Wearing baggy, suspendered pants and a hat many sizes too big, he stumbled across the stage, never losing a drop of his martini while constantly working magic with props from his pockets.

Drunk acts don't work well today, possibly due to changed attitudes toward alcoholism. But viewing his act in the context of its time, Hodge and I laughed ourselves to tears. While I rewound the film, Hodge told me that shortly before Bradford died, he had bequeathed his costume to the Fitch.

He turned on the video recorder, and we watched a tape of Siegfried and Roy early in their career. On the same cassette we also watched Blackstone Jr.'s routine where he invites audience members onstage to witness close-up the vanishing of a birdcage.

On another tape we watched Charles Kuralt do a report from the Fitch. Two unidentified magicians pulled scarves, flowers, cards, and even rabbits out of Kuralt's coat while he tried to carry on a conversation with them. At the end of the segment, he looked relieved to get back on the road again.

On film, we watched the opening of Thurston's stage show. His assistants turned the pages of a giant book, displaying pictures of history's greatest magicians. When they got to the last page, Thurston himself appeared.

I temporarily shoved thoughts of Perry Vaughn's death into a back corner of my mind. Feeling like a kid again, I yearned for a big box of popcorn, heavy on the butter. I wanted to chew gum and stick it under my seat when the taste died. I wanted to drink a giant ten-cent soda pop and bang the paper cup with my foot. The Thurston film ended all too quickly. I sure as hell didn't feel like doing what I knew I had to do. I let the white film leader flap around for several revolutions before I said, "Where's Bradford's costume?"

Hodge located the costume of the drunk-act magician without having to fire up his computer. Even before he opened its cardboard box, I smelled its pungent odor. Good.

"I want to borrow this," I said. "Just overnight." Hodge shrugged and said he couldn't see the harm.

I carried the box upstairs to the bar, and Hodge followed. While changing into the shabby, creased suit, I told him, "Check one of those crates behind the bar and see if Jack has any Pirate's Isle wine. Wait, that's not quite right. How about something cheaper, like Jester's Holiday? Two bottles, if there's any there."

It took me a few moments to find the secret pockets in the coat.

I put on the hat. It fit just fine, but an error like that probably wouldn't matter.

I folded my own clothes and asked Hodge to keep them for me.

He handed me the bottles of Jester's Holiday. Each label featured a white-faced mime in foolscap cavorting before fruit-colored footlights. How fitting. Still not certain if it was right, I opened one, poured some on my sleeve, and sniffed it as though shopping for expensive perfume.

"Just right."

I turned the bottle upside down and gave myself a shampoo. I chugged the remainder, toasting Hodge. "Life imitating art imitating life," I said.

He picked up the cardboard box containing my clothes and smiled, shaking his head.

I slipped the other bottle inside my coat pocket and walked outside—to continue my research.

CHAPTER FOURTEEN

I hadn't counted on a cellmate.

The deputy on night duty shoved me into one of the two holding cells in the sheriff's office. Playing true to role, I huddled unsteadily by my cell door, eyes half-closed. It was a full minute before I realized the other cell was occupied.

A deputy named Greene was working the graveyard shift. I was glad Sam Wirfel wasn't on duty. Showing no signs of recognizing me, Greene had treated me the same as any derelict picked up on a public-nuisance charge. I was about to try another residential section of Roselle when Greene finally pulled up in his squad car and asked me why I was singing and banging the garbage-can lids.

The deputy clanged shut my cell door and returned to the front office. He turned on a radio and tested five-second samplings of several stations before settling on one that featured phone calls from people whose problems were so overwhelming they couldn't tell them to anyone—except a talk-show host and thousands of listeners. The deputy's chair groaned as he tried to get comfortable.

The lockup's only illumination came from streetlights filtering through the cell windows. I almost broke character and stopped my slurred singing when I saw movement in the other cell. With eyes not yet accustomed to dimness, I could see him stretched out on a metal cot. He wore something glistening. A leather jacket.

"Hiya," I said. "How's the food here, partner?"

He lowered his head back to the pillow and stared at the ceiling. His eyes were shiny like his jacket.

I sat on my cot and rubbed my arms for warmth. The sheriff must have been saving taxpayers' dollars on the office heating bill. I sang softly, figuring my next move. Busting through the cell window (and the bars behind it) with a chisel and hacksaw would be an eight-hour job. Using picks and skill, walking out the cell door would take only thirty seconds. I'd have to wait for the deputy to go out on another call or until I heard him snoring. That wasn't my big problem.

My problem lay in the next cell—the man with the shiny eyes. Could I trust him?

For a half hour, he ignored my attempts at conversation. Even though my eyes had now adjusted to the dark, his face was still a shadowy blank. He got up once and paced briefly, but returned silently to his cot—at ease in darkness. Even when some of the street light hit his face during his stroll, it revealed no detail. A small man, he walked erect with deliberate, smooth movement. Showing no visible reaction, he kept watch on me. He was a man who didn't want to miss out on the world, but was unwilling to participate in it either.

I decided to drop my drunk act and speak clearly. "Is that what they pay that deputy for? Listening to the radio? Does he ever leave?"

My neighbor sat up, interested now. He waited for my next move. I gave him a good show.

I removed my cigarette pack from one of the secret compartments of Bradford's coat. I ripped up the two cigarettes that contained my picks. A final pick lay in the space between my cheek and my lower gum. I kneeled down beside my cot and bent one of the springs back and forth until I snapped a portion of it off.

Because of poor lighting, I had to rely on sound and touch, but I still made rapid progress. The man leaned forward on his cot. I now welcomed the cell's mild chill.

At normal room temperature the concentration would have left me sweat-soaked.

In a few minutes, my cell door swung open. After seeing that all my clacking and scraping wasn't desperate dreaming, the man moved to the front corner of his cell, nestling his face between the bars. Close-up, his eyes were steely. I was certain that he always looked directly at things, never at an angle. His hair in front swept down close to his eyebrows. His sideburns were long and cottony, giving way to black on the way up his face.

"You're good," he said. His voice was a benign growl.

"Thanks." I pulled the cell door back until it almost latched.

"I'm better," he said.

"Glad to hear it."

"If I'm so hot, you're probably wondering why I'm still here."

"Logical question."

"Logic don't exist in the stir, buddy, even in this tank town. You leave it in with the man out front, along with your wallet, belt, and shoelaces. Bet you had no wallet, though. Right?"

"Correct."

"I didn't think you'd have any ID with you. Gave him a false name, right?"

I nodded in agreement. He said, "You don't happen to be a friend of Georgie Hugo out of Elmira, do you?"

"No."

"I see. For a minute I thought he sent you here to spring me. A silly thought. I don't have any friends that close. I bet you're wondering right now what the hell to do with me."

"Yep."

"You've already figured I'm not going to raise hell over your springing the door, because that would mean trouble for me. You'd slam it shut before the deputy got back here, making me a liar. He'd have it in for me the rest of the night."

He thought for a moment. "Nope, you're thinking about tomorrow morning. When lard-ass Tarrant asks me why his lockup is shy one man. If I tell him the rummy next to me was a junior locksmith, the sheriff might get wise as to who you really are."

"You're doing good so far. Any suggestions about what I should do?"

"Not yet, but we got time on our hands right now. Did you sneak any money in with you? No, the kind of drunk you're playing wouldn't have more than small change. How about cigarettes? Got any left? I'll take only one right now, because I'll win the rest at poker."

He unzipped his jacket pocket, taking out a faded, warped deck and removing its rubber band. We both pulled our cots close to the bars.

He cleaned me out of cigarettes in a dozen hands. He wouldn't let me deal, dashing my chances for hanky-panky.

He said, "What time is it? Oh, I forgot. Bums don't need watches, right?"

"Yeah."

He held up a finger for me to be quiet, and we heard the talk-show host on the radio give the time. My poker partner said, "Almost two o'clock. We can move soon."

"Why at two?"

"Shhh."

The outside door to the office opened and shut. A few moments later, a nearby car started and drove off. The radio in the office played on.

"Girl friend?" I said.

He nodded. "Last night he was gone between two and three o'clock. You can figure on a half hour of safe time. Minimum."

"Half hour for what?"

"Don't play dumb. A half hour for your business, whatever it is. There's something you're itching to do out in that office, right?"

"What's the going price for lack of wisdom?" I already knew that answer.

"A limited partnership. You work. I keep watch. Then we both waltz out."

"Deal," I lied. Though my poker bluffs had failed, I didn't care whether he believed me now.

"How the hell did they nail a cookie like you?" I said.

"I was passing through this dump. Hell, it could have been any town, but the damn speed limit here is so low, I got a real good look at the sights. I saw this grocery store that looked closed. I let myself in and discovered how wrong I was. The owner popped out from behind the lunch cakes and shoved a gun under my nose, telling me not to breathe. When the sheriff finally showed up to arrest me, I gave him a false name. I never carry genuine ID."

"You didn't resist?"

"With two guns pointed at me? No way."

I asked the man if the sheriff had a Band-Aid on his head when he showed up.

"Yeah. He did."

"After he locked you up, what did Sheriff Tarrant do?"

"He used the phone, talking low so I couldn't hear him. Someone else arrived, and there was more talking. I heard a funny rolling sound that reminded me of a wheelbarrow. A door inside the office opened and closed. Then they both left."

"There wasn't anybody else locked up since you've been in here?"

"No, you're my first neighbor."

I started to exit when he grabbed me with both hands and pulled me so hard my forehead bounced on the bars.

"Remember the deal," he said, face pressed to mine. His smile was two rows of straight, sharp white.

He let go. I walked out of my cell and into the office before he shouted. "What about me?"

"You watch the back. From out here, I can hear anything suspicious out front. If I have to run, there'll be only one of us to get back in the cell. When I'm done with my business, I'll let you out."

I intended to keep him locked up, fearing that the deputy

would return to find two empty cells and one dead magician in his office.

Two desks, a photocopier, a computer terminal, and three file cabinets filled most of the office. There were two doors on either side of the file cabinets. I tried one door and couldn't get it entirely open because the computer terminal blocked it. This door led nowhere—just a cubbyhole closet for all the hats and coats people took with them when going "downtown" with Tarrant. The other door opened into a room with a table and three chairs, probably where Tarrant conducted interviews.

I turned off the radio and listened to the traffic outside.

"Everything okay out there?" the prisoner said.

"Yeah."

The cabinets were unlocked. In the top drawer I found my bottle of Jester's Holiday. In the drawer below that I located Perry Vaughn's file. I flipped through the pages. Not surprisingly, it was thick, a detailed account of his brushes with the law, but with no mention of his final brush. The documents concerning his death were elsewhere. On one desk was a photo of a blue-haired woman with a cold smile whom I figured to be Tarrant's wife. There were no pictures of children. I tried the drawers. Locked.

I reached for my picks. Not in my left pocket. My right? No. Oh shit. I turned around, knowing what I'd see.

My jailmate stood in the doorway, savoring the expression on my face. He displayed a lock pick in either hand.

When had he—?

"When you grabbed me, right?" I asked.

"When else?"

It was the same way I had earlier duped Tarrant. I got out of the way so he'd have a clear path to the door, and I hoped he'd entertain no violent thoughts along the way.

"I ain't going nowhere yet," he said, eyeing the open cabinet. "Looking for a file? Probably in chubby's desk. Catch."

I caught one pick, but missed the other and had to search on the floor for it. While I was doing that, he took the third one out of his pocket and opened Tarrant's desk drawer with no wasted movement. He was right; he was better than me.

The contents of Tarrant's desk made Hodge's meticulous cataloguing system seem like a landfill. All the pencils were rapier-sharp, all pointing in the same direction with the brand name facing up. Thumbtacks were stuck in a rectangle of cardboard, grouped in formation according to color. They were pretty. The paper clips lay side by side in a holder that would dispense one gleaming clip at a time. In one corner of the drawer was a book of matches. Its red musical notes and champagne bubbles looked familiar. I picked it up and saw that the cover said "Torme's."

"Fifty-two," the man said.

"What?"

"There are fifty-two paper clips in this desk." He handed me a file card on which Tarrant kept a running inventory of every item in his desk. Everything.

"Where'd you get this card? If you don't put it back in exactly the same place, he's going to know we went through his desk."

He put it back. While I stared in disbelief at the neatness-gone-mad in Tarrant's desk, the man found Vaughn's folder in a lower drawer.

I took back the last pick and put all them in my coat. The man continued looking through the sheriff's desk. He removed another file. It was thin and new-looking.

"Mine," he said. "It goes with me."

He handed me yet one more folder. "This was on top. There's a bunch like that in there," he said. "No label on the outside."

I opened the folder. It was the case file on an unsolved hit-and-run death of an eight-year-old girl.

He looked at the wall clock and said, "I still don't know who you are, but if you're serious about not tipping your identity, you'd better not take any files with you." He looked at the copy machine and said, "We got time."

After a few false starts, we got the machine to produce

readable copies. He fed it while I stacked the originals and the copies, resisting the temptation to slow down and read them.

"You're not as nervous as a few minutes ago," he said.

"Yeah. I realize now that violent types don't take the pains to learn to use picks the way you do."

When we finished, we put everything back. Except ourselves.

I turned the radio back on.

The man said, "You got me out of a jam, and I'm grateful. Of course, I don't carry a business card, but there's a guy in Philadelphia named Ryder. Ask for him at the Tobark tobacco shop. He can connect us if you ever need a partner."

I went back into the holding area, turned on the lights, made sure I hadn't left anything, and locked the cell doors. I noticed for the first time all the pencil and ink scrawlings on the walls. Most were humorless, vulgar messages. The drawings were all crude in both style and content. Except for one. It was a detailed rendering of a nude brunette standing in an aggressively sexy bodybuilder's pose. A tattoo of a bird was on the lower part of one buttock. Michelle Blue. A legacy from Perry Vaughn during one of his visits.

I returned to the office. The prisoner was gone.

A car door slammed. The deputy?

I slipped into the closet, hoping he wouldn't want to hang up his jacket.

I heard the deputy enter, walking cautiously to the holding tank. The lights. I had forgotten turn them off. He'd have his gun drawn, for sure. I thrust open the closet, bouncing the door off the computer terminal. I made a noisy dash and was outside before I heard the deputy start cursing, mourning the possible loss of his job.

Holding my sheaf of papers tight, I jogged into the same darkness that had already absorbed one criminal thus far that night.

CHAPTER FIFTEEN

I expected sirens and flashing lights at any moment during my trek back to the Fitch. A midnight cabdriver pulled up beside me. He was desperate for a fare, even from an out-of-breath drunk with a stack of papers under his arm and a bottle under the other. I wanted a lift, but had only a dollar in change on me. I had dressed the part too well.

I stopped at a closed gas station and got a pack of peanut-butter crackers and a can of soda from a vending machine. Dinner. I also paid a visit to my van and picked up a few things that would make me more comfortable in my new room.

Back in the basement of the Fitch, Gregory Hodge was still pecking at his computer. I wondered how serious Hodge was about the competition. Was he here only for the opportunity to explore the basement memorabilia? Or for some other reason?

I scooped up my box of clothing from the floor beside him and hurried upstairs before he asked questions.

Three-thirty A. M. was too late to tell Cate what I had accomplished. She needed all the rest she could get.

I chose a sixth-floor room. All the ones above the second, where the clowns were staying, were barren. No furniture or curtains. No heat, either. Jack must have shut off the ducts to the unoccupied rooms. The electricity and water still worked, not to mention a phone that gave me a friendly dial tone when I picked it up. I didn't want to risk any light being spotted from the street, yet I didn't want to wait for daylight to read. I draped my blanket across the window. For now, I contented myself with shivering and staying as motionless as I could in my sleeping bag while reading the Vaughn file by flashlight. I kept thinking about the jail cell and that prisoner I had helped escape. Not all my shivers were from the cold.

I ate the last cracker and drank what remained of my bottle of Jester's Holiday. Mixing it with diet soda made a rancid taste, and it burned going down. Although no substitute for my blanket, I welcomed the warm feeling.

I learned nothing new from the file on Vaughn's death. It was sketchy and hastily written, while Coroner Theodore Crowell's preliminary autopsy report was clear and concise. I found no grammatical or typographical errors unless, of course, they were in the medical terminology.

After rigor mortis had subsided, they extricated Vaughn's body from the safe, removing his makeup. The postmortem was performed at a local funeral home owned by Garth Eyles. The nearest big medical center was fifty-five miles away, and the report justified the autopsy site by listing the qualifications of the M.E. Crowell's credentials surprised me. In many communities as small as Roselle, the coroner often is an elected official with little, if any, medical background. Crowell was a qualified medical examiner whose academic background was as formidable as it was lengthy.

I finished the document, puzzling over the sections that relied on medical jargon, but regretting when I did understand all too clearly some of the more gruesome details. Asphyxiation was the official cause of death.

I don't know about you, but usually after I get myself arrested, bust out, eat a full-course dinner, and read an autopsy report, I don't feel much like turning in. I set the beeper on my wrist watch for seven A.M., but I wasn't the least drowsy.

I wanted to talk to someone. I picked up the phone, dialed a nine, and got the outside dial tone. Information gave me the number of Jimbo's Pizza.

When Jimbo's answered, I said, "Do you deliver to the Fitch?"

"Sure. What size and what's on it?"

"Are you the only place in Roselle that makes night deliveries?"

"Yeah."

"How many deliverymen work the night shift?"

"Just one. Things are slack at this hour. What size and what—"

"Your deliveryman's there right now?"

"Yeah."

"You never deliver yourself?"

"Ever hear of division of labor? Since I talk good and make great dough, I stay here and take the calls. Buster looks good in person and doesn't mind beating up his Camaro and giving it a permanent tomato-sauce smell, so he does deliveries."

"Can I talk to Buster?"

"First, what size and what do you want on it?"

I ordered their most expensive pie, thereby earning the right to talk to Buster.

"Buster, I'd like to ask a few questions about deliveries to the Fitch."

The dough man was right. Buster was ill at ease and inarticulate over the phone. I let him take his time answering my questions.

While waiting for Buster to deliver the pizza, I picked up the copies I had made of the hit-and-run report. The deceased's name was Dorinda Bradley, and she had been eight years old. A physician from out of town, not Ted Crowell, performed the autopsy. The directory assistance operator gave me Crowell's number. I called and got his answering service. I identified myself as a lawyer from Baltimore and told the lady I'd be calling later for information on the Dorinda Bradley case.

After hanging up, I realized I still wanted to talk to

someone, preferably a beautiful woman. Now, what beautiful women did I know in Roselle?

Taking the chance she might now be up, I dialed Cate's number. Her phone rang twice.

"Hello."

"I didn't wake you?"

"No."

"Worried?"

"No, Spillman's scheduled a fairly easy day tomorrow."

"I mean worried about me."

"Not at all."

I told her what happened at the jail.

"If you had told me what you were planning, I'd have helped."

"I didn't want to involve you in a felony."

"Any valuable information in the files?"

I told her what I'd learned, and that I was glad Spillman hadn't planned a rigorous day for tomorrow.

"What do you have in mind?" she asked.

"How would you like to visit a funeral parlor?"

"Sounds cheery."

"How did Jack's search go? Don't tell me. He discovered that someone's been staying in one of the vacant rooms. Number 545. Right?"

"Hey, that's right. How did you know?"

"A pizza man told me."

"But how—what was that? Did you hear that?"

"What?"

She dropped the phone. I heard her faint voice say, "Who's out there? Are you all right?"

Over the phone, I heard a man yell in pain. I hung up and went for the door, regretting the distance I had placed between me and the occupied rooms.

I startled Cate when I lunged through the stairwell door. She was kneeling in the hallway beside Gregory Hodge, who was sitting with his back to the wall. Two red looseleaf notebooks lay beside him. One of his eyes was badly swollen. It was red and on its way to becoming black. He was conscious but confused, so I gave him a minute to realize that he wasn't badly hurt and would live to collect magic for many more years.

Novak and Spillman looked on. They were in their pajamas, Novak in slippers and Spillman in his bare feet. Not fully awake yet, they nervously shifted from foot to foot, wanting to help but not knowing how.

Farther down the hall stood an impassive Rupeka. He wore poppy-colored bikini shorts. Nothing else.

I'm not sure what did more to render these three speechless—Hodge's injury or the sight of Cate ministering to him. They had grown used to seeing her in her shapeless, asexual Quimp costume and her baggy sweatpants. Now she wore a hot-pink negligee whose lace was so delicate it seemed in the midst of dissolving. She was fascinating to look at when she was still. Doubly so when she moved.

When I saw Hodge's eyes stop wandering and focus in on Cate, I asked him what happened.

He mulled over the question before answering. "After finishing downstairs, I walked up here. When I opened the stairwell door, someone rapped me from the side. I put my hands over my eyes, so I didn't get a look at him."

Besides the eye, I saw that he had also taken a shot to his head, above the ear.

"He hit you twice?" I said.

"Just once, in the eye. I bumped my head going down. If I hadn't been carrying these notebooks, I would have had better balance." His body stiffened upon remembering his notes. He snatched up one of the looseleaf notebooks, but I picked the other up before he did.

"Did you have any other notebooks?"

"Yes. One more." He tried getting up, but Rupeka moved in and pushed him back down. I walked up the hall and checked the stairway.

"It's gone," I said when I returned.

I leafed through the notebook in my hands. Most of the

pages were handwritten, but some were printout from his computer. His writing wasn't pretty, but every word was legible and the margins were straight—the kind of notes I loved to borrow after skipping college classes. Skimming through, I found nothing other than data on the magic history of the hotel.

"Why would someone want your notes enough to hurt you?" I asked. "Are they valuable?"

"Not to anyone but me," he said, brushing Rupeka's helping hand off his shoulder.

"No secret maps to show where lost treasures in the hotel are hidden?" Novak said, smiling.

"No treasures. These notes aren't even the actual catalogue of the holdings. I'm recording all that on computer disks downstairs." Hodge put his hands flat on the floor. "I think I can get up now, but I've got to do it slowly." Shooing away assistance from Rupeka and Cate, he stood without wavering.

"Is the collection itself valuable?" I asked.

"Yes, somewhat, but Fort Knox it's not. No one item down there is worth more than a few hundred. That stuff would be hard to fence, since most of it is unique. Any used-magic dealer would know where it came from."

"People get mugged for much less," I said.

"I don't like that eye," Rupeka said. "Better get it checked at a hospital."

"I'll be fine, with rest. I've been burning the candle at both ends, with the cataloguing and the competition. Now I have an excuse to get a little more sleep."

We all looked to Spillman, who was silent for a long while. He finally gave in and said, "Why, uh, yes. Gregory should definitely take the morning off."

Cate looked again at Hodge's eye, the bottom now bordered by a purple crescent. She glared at Spillman. "Just the *morning* off?"

"I actually meant that he's excused from *all* proceedings tomorrow," Spillman said.

"That's okay," Hodge said. "Just slacking off my cataloguing activities will give me plenty of rest. I'll see you all at the afternoon session.''

I returned Hodge's other notebook, and he trudged into his room, looking like a drunk pretending not to have had too many.

Spillman and Novak returned to their rooms, but Rupeka lingered.

''Did you hear anything?'' I asked.

''Only his yell. It woke me up,'' he said. ''No footsteps or other voices. No slamming door. Oh, I know what you're thinking. The attacker could have been one of us? Right?''

''Yeah,'' I said.

''Why? Just for a notebook?''

''That and possibly more.''

''What?''

''You heard Hodge. This incident might scare him away from working in the basement for a while.''

''Someone's afraid he's going to stumble across something damaging to them?'' Cate said.

''Or that he already has,'' Rupeka said. ''I'd like to see what's in that missing notebook.''

''Me too,'' I said. ''One more thing, what do you make of his head injury?''

''Not serious, but he didn't get that from falling.''

''I agree,'' I said.

''Then how?'' Cate asked.

''Hodge lied,'' Rupeka said. ''He did get punched, but he also got kicked after he went down. He's scared to admit how vicious the attack really was.'' He looked down at his feet as if to underscore that they were bare, thus making it less likely that he delivered that kick.

''See you tomorrow. Get some sleep,'' he said and went inside his room.

''Tried to make a point about his feet, didn't he?'' Cate said as I walked her back to her room.

''Doesn't mean a thing.''

''Why?''

"During police training, he surely received martial-arts instruction."

"Kicking with bare feet," she said.

"Exactly."

"What about one of the others?"

"Who was in the hall when you rushed out?" I asked.

"Just Hodge and Rupeka. A minute later, Spillman and Novak appeared. Oh, I see. If Novak was startled out of sleep, how did he have time to put on slippers?"

"Another suspect," I said.

We stopped at her door. It was still ajar. I noted how her negligee barely covered her hips. The design on the front was lacy flowers joined at the middle by a vertical row of pill-size buttons that looked as though a gentle breeze could undo them. I liked that illusion and spent a pleasant moment trying to conjure up a breeze. Some magic is beyond even my realm.

Footsteps and coughing came from the stairway, and a man wearing trousers and no shirt stepped into the hall. His pale belly bobbed in rhythm to his walk. It was Jack, and he must have heard the commotion from his suite on the third floor. He didn't have his gun.

"Something happen here?"

"Action's over. You missed it."

Or had he? Cate tried her best to keep her eyes off Jack's feet. He wore unshined wing tips. Laced neat and tight.

I told him about Hodge's ambush.

When I finished, Jack said, "It was that son of a bitch living in 545, wasn't it?"

Jack was still angry that I insisted we wait in the lobby for Buster, the pizza man. He was also insulted that I wouldn't reveal the number of the room I was now staying in.

When Buster showed up, Jack said, "Who the hell eats pizza at four A.M.?"

"The man in Room 545 did," Buster said.

When he delivered Cate's pizza the other night, he had

indicated that he made deliveries to someone on one of the upper floors. Jack had said that all the rooms above the second floor were unoccupied, but it hadn't struck me as odd at the time.

I paid Buster for the pizza and asked him what he knew about Mr. Five-Four-Five.

"The guy was weird, but three more customers like him and I could've retired early. I knew he was too good to be true."

"What was weird about him?" I said.

"When I'd leave his order on the floor in front of his room, the money was always waiting for me, usually a big bill. His instructions on the phone were to keep the change. Hey, for that kind of dough, I didn't care how goofy he was."

"When did you start his deliveries?"

"Thursday. The last was early Monday morning. No calls after that. If you find him, tell him I'll deliver anytime."

"Did he ever give a name?"

"No."

"Always early morning?" I asked.

"Always. Between three o'clock and four-thirty."

"You can't describe him?"

"Never saw him. Just the color of his money."

"Did he ever buy anything other than food? Ask you to run errands?"

"Once I picked up something at a pharmacy and brought it back the next night."

"Drugs?" Jack said.

"No. Skin ointment. Must have had a rash or something."

"Maybe," I said. When I tipped him, Buster tried not to look hurt at the amount, but he knew it would be ages before he found another customer like the man in 545.

Both Cate and Jack insisted on accompanying me up to 545. They didn't want any of the pizza, so I carried the box along.

Five-forty-five was a duplicate of my current room: no furniture or curtains. However, this room was very lived in. The dates on newspapers piled in the corner supported the pizza man's claim of when the room was occupied. The secret tenant left plenty behind, but no identification. The closet contained four suits and two coats, all with tailor's label on them, but none with personal initials. His luggage was worn, but he had paid top dollar for it. Food wrappers and pizza boxes stuck out of the waste can. There were no ticket stubs, receipts, or notes. No wallet.

In the bathroom we found a tube of skin ointment, squeezed flat, along with a square of cardboard that had once held pharmaceutical capsules in plastic bubbles. The label said Dadrium.

"Think he'll be back?" Cate asked.

"No," I said. "Not to this room. Judging from when he stopped sending out for food and from the last date on those newspapers, I'd say the death of Perry Vaughn has scared him off. There is a small possibility he's staying in another room and taking more care to conceal his presence. He might have been Hodge's attacker."

"We could do another room-to-room search tomorrow," Jack said.

I studied the pill container.

"No, hold off on the search, Jack. I want to check with a medical authority about these capsules."

"The M.E.?" Cate asked.

"Yeah," I said. "Maybe him, too."

CHAPTER SIXTEEN

It looked like an April day, but felt like March. I turned my back on the bullying wind and tried to zip my jacket. My hands felt like clumsy paws. I worried that Cate hadn't dressed warmly enough, either.

I walked up the street past the funeral home. When I was sure I wasn't being watched, I cut across a vacant lot and up an embankment thick with dry brush. As the brush gave way to trees, I slowed down. The glint from the binoculars made Cate easy to spot, but I hoped the undertaker was too preoccupied to notice.

With her early-morning clown session behind her, Cate was now posing as a bird-watcher, albeit a lazy one. She sat on a blanket under the chestnut tree on the hill behind the Garth Eyles Mortuary. Her jacket didn't look much heavier than a blouse. A scarf covered her neck, but it too looked inadequate. Elbows planted on raised knees, she made minute adjustments to the binoculars' focus.

It was my idea for her to have a clipboard and pen, but the ornithology book costing seventeen ninety-five was her brainstorm. Although she agreed that it was unlikely she'd be spotted, let alone be questioned, she had still insisted on the book for, as she called it, inner authenticity. Oh boy. Method actors.

Her eyes stayed pressed to the lenses. I thought she didn't hear me approach, but then she slid the clipboard my way. I picked it up and read her unsteady writing. She had either hired an infant to take notes, or she had written without looking down. She had been keeping watch here for well over an hour.

"If concentration is the only thing that counts, you've got this clown competition in your pocket," I said. "I need some translation here. Your abbreviations have me baffled."

"Not much to tell. Eyles has been doing a lot of housework. He's either single or his wife works. He answered the phone twice. At—"

"Ten-twenty and ten twenty-two, if p on your notes stands for phone."

I consulted my own notepad. On it was written "10:20"—the time I had made my call to the mortician.

"What happened at the medical examiner's?" she said.

"In the hour between making my appointment and arriving, something urgent came up for Crowell. He was out, and his receptionist was vague about his return. She let me use her phone, though."

"To call our funeral director here?"

"Right. I made sure the receptionist overheard the conversation. I asked Eyles if he had handled the funeral arrangements for Perry Vaughn. He said Vaughn's body has already been sent for cremation. He didn't sound shook until I said I would be visiting shortly with specific questions about the condition of the body. After leaving, I waited outside for a ten count and went back in. The receptionist was on the phone. Her tongue got all tied when she saw me again."

Cate said, "After Eyles got off the phone with Crowell's receptionist, he made a quick phone call. He shook his hand in the air, as though he were talking to someone right in front of him. He hung up so hard I practically heard the bell way up here." She stood up, binoculars still growing out of her eyes. "Uh-oh. We'd better get moving. He's putting his coat on. Hey, what's that on his belt—a gun?"

"Let me see." She gave me the binoculars. She had used them so long, her eyes were ringed, reminding me of raccoon's. I looked through the binoculars and said, "No, that's a pocket pager he's wearing. Does he think more mortuary business is coming his way? Hope it's nobody we know.''

I handed back the glasses. ''He's left his office and will be outside—''

Cate pointed at Eyles, heading briskly toward his car, his black topcoat billowing behind him. He got in and backed out of his driveway.

I said, ''He's heading west toward Wallace Avenue.''

She looked at me questioningly.

''Sheriff Tarrant's office is on Wallace Avenue,'' I said.

By the time we folded the blanket and walked down the hill to my van, Eyles was out of sight. We got on Wallace and drove eight blocks up to Tarrant's office. The mortician's black sedan was parked in front.

''You really scared him,'' Cate said.

We parked farther up the street and waited.

He was still inside an hour later, so we decided to return to the Fitch. Cate had an afternoon clown session to prepare for. I was expecting a call at three o'clock from my favorite psychiatrist.

Instead of going inside with Cate, I lingered in front of the hotel entrance, confident that nobody would mistake me for the doorman. I wore jeans, faded to the shade of a blueberry milkshake, and a silky shirt covered with a swirling print of jungle vegetation. My shirt cuffs were folded back over my jacket sleeves, and my lapels hung outside my jacket. Hang a few pounds of gold around my neck, and my costume would have been just right to play street barker for a nude dance club.

As a child, I was intrigued with costumes long before I took up magic, Halloween being my favorite holiday. There were several costumes in my professional wardrobe, but I usually wore only two: a black tux (for square audiences) and a high-necked, sequined suit, circa Elvis 1975 (for square audiences that thought they were hip). Tomorrow night, if I could persuade the *Magazine Tonite* people to

come the Roselle post office, I'd wear my sequined suit—
and do my damndest to keep a straight face.

Ten minutes went by. The only vehicles were those driv-
en by the wrecking crew. The only pedestrian I saw was a
man approaching from a block away, carrying a paper bag.
As he got closer, I saw it was Novak. No mistaking his
snappy pace and erect posture. His walk resembled a dou-
ble-time parade march. No fancy Phil Fleming exercise
equipment for this man. I could picture him in the morning,
stuffing himself with vitamins, turning his stomach inside
out with situps, and finishing himself off with a few light-
ning minutes with a jump rope, his most intricate piece of
fitness apparatus.

When he spotted me, his pace slackened. If he had considered avoiding me, I saw no reluctance in his face. He
greeted me with a rich smile. His cheeks had so much color
they were glossy. The gusty wind tossed his hair, but when
when the air died down, every silver strand returned to its
assigned post. He wore no coat, only a long-sleeved shirt
with red candy stripes. It had epaulets on the shoulders and
metal snaps instead of buttons. The top two snaps were
undone.

Most people would have praised him on how healthy he
looked, how his age didn't show, and how he mocked the
elements by undressing for the season. Not me. I lit up a
cigarette and offered him one. He looked at me as though
I had waved a knife in his face.

I noticed that his hammer-banged thumb now appeared
healed. I was glad that I hadn't bet him the two hundred.
He held it up for me to see, but I pretended not to notice.

Novak positioned himself away from where the breeze
was carrying my smoke. He watched the dust clouds waft
from the windows of the Edison Office Building. Men were
making numerous trips in and out, and I heard the sounds
of prying wood. "Making progress, aren't they?" he said.

"Yep. After the Edison, it'll be the Fitch."

"Before I left today, I checked out that building. The

cornerstone says it was built in the twenties and was originally a bank. It probably failed during the Depression.''

I nodded. Seeing me stare at his bag, he opened it up and revealed its contents. I felt like a customs agent.

He said, ''I visited an athletic store uptown. I decided to walk rather than drive, giving myself a nice warmup for this afternoon's session. I bought some protective pads for me and Hodge.''

He displayed elbow and knee pads of various sizes.

''Spillman fielding a touch football team?'' I asked.

''No. These are for the acrobatics.''

An internal alarm clanged, and I saw an image of Cate in a cast.

''Acrobatics?'' I said. ''It's been seven years since Quimp's performed acrobatics in his show. He still does one elementary cartwheel, exquisitely, but it's a far cry from what he used to do. Does Cate know about this?''

Novak shrugged.

''Hodge shouldn't be doing flips in his condition.''

Novak tried on an elbow pad and smiled with patient condescension. ''Give us credit, Colderwood. You don't have a monopoly on amazing feats. None of us is exactly doddering. I've overcome more severe obstacles than a few somersaults.''

''I see. Simply imagine that you're eighteen, and your body will behave accordingly? Many a time I've begged Eros to temporarily give me back my teenage bod. Each time I had to be content with reality, which isn't all that bad, let me tell you. But I don't agree with your philosophy. We all have limits.''

''But nobody agrees precisely what the limits of human performance are. Need I point this out to a man who catches bullets in his teeth and escapes from locked chains in icy rivers?''

''I'm afraid my water escapes are history, like Quimp's acrobatics. Though dangerous, my escapes were all trickery—carefully calculated risks. Because a misguided few might believe I had supernatural powers, I prefaced each stunt with a speech that credited illusion, not the occult, for my success."

"What about your bullet-catching? Surely that is—"

"—a magic trick, accomplished by gimmickry that's no more impressive than Quimp's water-shooting flower. If it were more than pure show biz, don't you think that the U.S. Military would have offered me a contract by now? Novak, let me assure you: try catching a bullet in your teeth without the aid of the magician's skill, and you'll incur great dental expense."

"Surely there are some paranormal phenomena you believe in. How about the Eastern meditators who levitate?"

"Ever see any?"

"No."

"When you do, take some photos for me. Just make sure you're far enough away to show the trampoline that the floatee is bouncing on. People like you worry me, Novak. I don't know what scares me more—that some people swallow what you say, or that maybe you actually believe it yourself."

His expression reminded me of a politician glad to be asked a question he had prepped for. "Enjoy those cigarettes?"

I was so absorbed in the conversation that I had unconsciously ground out my first Lucky and lit another.

"Your answer's written on your face," he said. "If you hate them, why not quit?"

"I suppose you have a magic cure—some pill or potion that costs only forty-nine ninety-five, right?"

"Not magical. Scientific—like all my claims. If you're game, you can try it later."

He jammed his athletic padding back into the bag and walked past me. At the hotel entrance, he turned and said, "Colderwood, you have no imagination."

"Oh, yeah? I admit I was first on my block to get wise to the Santa Claus scam, but I kept mum to my friends about the bad news. Know why? I couldn't see where it hurt them. The same goes for you, Novak If you're harming people, I'll tell the world—*loud*. I promise. Maybe it's time I read some of your books.''

I extended my hand for him to shake. ''Hey, don't go away mad,'' I said. He cautiously shook my hand. I reached for his left and made it a double handshake. The joybuzzer concealed in my hand went off, and he jerked away as if receiving a real electric shock. Who says I don't have imagination?

As the door to the Fitch hissed shut behind him, I wondered how badly he wanted to be the new Quimp and whether he'd hurt anyone for that honor. Like Gregory Hodge or Perry Vaughn.

I looked down at my hand. It was stained with flesh-tone makeup. Novak had healed his thumb, all right. Cosmetically.

CHAPTER SEVENTEEN

Keeping my word, I walked four blocks up the street to a drugstore and bought Novak's latest paperback, *Laughter, the Healthy O.D.* The cover showed Novak slapping his raised thigh and contorting his face with laughter. Because of the laughter, I barely recognized him.

Back in the hotel lobby, all the clowns except for Cate had their chairs pulled close while Novak enchanted them with the tale of when he dreamed the winning numbers in a state lottery seven days in a row and then donated the money to charity. I had heard him tell that one on TV and didn't care for a rehash. If I wanted to refresh my memory, I'd look it up in his book.

I met Cate as she came out of the hotel office. Feeling like an atheist toting a Bible, I covered Novak's book with my hand.

She said, "I've got to change. Spillman changed the program for this afternoon."

"I heard. Acrobatics, right?"

She nodded. "I'll wear dance leotards and jogging shoes."

"Cate, is this still worth it? The contest is getting screwier by the day. And riskier. Novak thinks he's Clark Kent, Rupeka's playing bodyguard by carrying a gun, and Hodge has already gotten hurt. We still don't know what all this has to do with Perry Vaughn. Why pretend this is as important as a major film role?"

Chairs rustled as the would-be clowns got up. They

formed a line, and Spillman led them in stretching exercises. Only Novak could duplicate Spillman's contortions. The groaning Hodge and Rupeka only performed rough abbreviations of the movements.

"I'm late," Cate said. She took a thin, bound booklet from her purse and handed it to me. Her acting portfolio. "If you find anything I've done in here that's more important than this contest, let me know."

"Is day after tomorrow still okay for the—?"

"You and I won't have much time to rehearse. You'd better think twice about your risks, too. Look, I've got to go. I haven't even coasted yet today. There were some phone calls for you. I left the messages on the office desk."

Coasted?

As she went upstairs, I opened Novak's book to the glossary. "Coast," according to Novak, was ". . . a state of equanimity similar to the initial stages of meditation." I shook my head, feeling betrayed (and jealous) that Cate was buying Novak's baloney.

I closed the office door to shut out Spillman's singsong counting of his exercises. Three phone messages were written on file cards, clipped together. Two were in Cate's handwriting; the other in Jack's. I spread them out onto the desk.

Dr. Randy Pescatore had called twice, and Jeffers once. Pescatore left a phone number, while Jeffers left only a taunt.

Jeffers's message said, "Don't combine two inevitables. See you soon." Below, Jack wrote: "Harry, who is this guy? He scares me."

I crumpled the card and tossed it in the wastebasket. I dialed Pescatore's number, knowing I'd have to let it ring a long time. Feet propped on the desk and chair tilted back on two legs, I lit a cigarette and made great efforts to enjoy it. I thought of Novak's self-righteous offer to end, for an unspecified fee, my nicotine slavery. After three unpleasant puffs, I ground out the butt in the ashtray. Pescatore's number rang on.

I opened Cate's résumé. Page one featured a eight-by-ten head-and-shoulders shot that captured her surface beauty but not her personality.

On the following page were statistics that were supposed to be the essence of one Cate Elliott Fleming, actress: height; weight; and measurements for bust, waist, hips, thighs, and calves. The numbers were as meaningless to me as Hodge's computer entries.

I leafed through the next pages, treating myself to photos of Cate in bathing suits, evening gowns, and lingerie. There was even a fog-filter shot of her stepping from a steamy shower. Fine, I thought, if her sole ambition was to continue modeling for mail-order catalogs.

One page was a montage of Cates. Old Cate, ugly Cate, funny Cate, stupid Cate, and just plain Cate. All calculated for producers to say, "Damn, what role *can't* this woman play?"

After all this buildup, the last page meekly listed her credits—a synopsis of the years following our separation. Triple spacing only drew attention to the sparseness of her acting experience. Summer stock and a summary of modeling experience padded the list. There was no mention of her being a magician's assistant.

The geographic limitations of her work stunned me. The first year after quitting our act, she worked widely. In the later years, she got fewer jobs outside of New England, none in New York. Her West Coast work had totally dried up. Almost as if—

"Hello. WGHI, the Station for Conversation. First name, sex, and age, please."

Still gazing at the résumé, I gave him the information.

"Your first name is Merlin?" the man asked.

"Yes."

"In one sentence, what is your problem?"

I closed Cate's portfolio and said, "I think I'm in love

with a married woman—an actress. I'm sure she doesn't care much for me."

"Fine. If you'll hold—"

"I'm also close to going broke."

"Thank you. If—"

"Maybe I'm paranoic, but I think someone wants to kill me. One man's already dead, and another has been attacked. I can't even trust the sheriff. He could be the one that's after me."

"Hold, please. Don't hang up. Whatever you do."

For a long minute I listened to sweet background music. Finally a familiar voice said, "Harry, what the hell did you say to Benny, my screener?"

"That you, Randy? Oh, I didn't say much. Just some minor details of my life. Why?"

I could hear the chirping of rewinding audio tape behind Dr. Randy Pescatore's voice. Pescatore, a psychiatrist in a small Pennsylvania town, once helped me when I was hired by a widow to find out if her husband really committed suicide.

"The way Benny flailed his arms, I thought you were the Soda Pop Killer confessing," he said.

"The what?"

"A local serial murderer. You've probably never heard of him. His victim count isn't high enough yet for widespread coverage."

I didn't know there was such a magic number. If so, I hoped it was never made public.

Pescatore said to his screener, "Sorry, Benny, he's a friend. What's that? . . . I'll tell him. Harry, Benny's disappointed. He said you could have been the best caller this month."

"Why a radio show, Randy? Or should I, like your listeners, call you *Doctor* Randy?"

It was hard to imagine Pescatore advising divorces, giving sexual advice, and consoling depressed parents while thousands listened.

"It's an experiment. We're ending our third and final month. If we win our market share, they'll renew us."

In the background, over theme music, an announcer closed out another day of "The Dr. Randy Show."

"Market share? That's agent talk," I said.

"You're right, I *do* have an agent, and maybe he could use an over-the-hill magician in his stable. I'll ask him. Seriously, Harry, I know I'm reaching people who'd never see a shrink in person, but feel comfortable with the anonymity of radio."

"I know what you mean," I said. And then I started down my list of questions.

"One at a time," he said. "I got your message when I arrived this morning, and I checked on most of your questions. First, that ointment you inquired about was, until recently, available only by prescription. It's used primarily for treatment of minor burns. That other drug, Dadrium, is a tranquilizer."

"How tranquil will it make you? For instance, if life was getting me down and the only thing that would pick me up would be committing a major crime, would a few hits of Dadrium help me overcome my nerve problems?"

"Maybe. I called Crown Laboratories, the manufacturer of Dadrium. Three salesmen service the Roselle region."

"Salesmen?"

"Yeah. Dadrium is brand-new. The package you found was most likely a sample. Crown said most of the samples would still be in the hands of their sales force."

He read the names of the three salesmen. Number three was Lloyd Ames. I pointed out its similarity to James Loy, the only person registered at the Fitch whom Cate couldn't track down.

"You're not interested in the psychology behind why people choose phony names similar to their real ones, are you?"

"Another time," I said.

He gave me Ames's address and phone number. Crown

hadn't hesitated releasing that information to Pescatore, a medical doctor and potential customer.

"You must be mixed up in a doozy, Harry."

"Why do you say that?"

"Your other two questions make a weird juxtaposition. You wanted my opinion of Teddy Crowell *and* Lorenz Novak. Crowell is the M.E. down there in Roselle, right?"

"Teddy? He's a friend of yours?"

"He always used Teddy in his byline. I've never met Crowell, but I've read all his old journal articles. Twice."

"How does an authority in forensic pathology end up in Roselle?"

"Retirement and a drinking problem that he has, at best, held at bay. After thirty years of manning a medical examiner's office in upstate New York, he packed it in and bought a house near Roselle. Like a lot of retirees, he couldn't stay idle, so, at election time, he ran for coroner. The community's lucky to have him. The pay's probably next to nothing."

"And Novak?"

Pescatore whistled. "If my mike were on, I'd tell the listeners how Lorenz Novak has aided physicians in alerting patients to their own responsibility in the healing process."

"But your mike's off."

He made quacking noises.

"Why not tell the truth?" I said.

"I base my opinion upon what Novak *implies* in his writing. Plenty of research backs up his claims that a patient with a positive drive recuperates faster than a whiny one, and that a slew of good things happen physiologically when we laugh. I don't quarrel with his surface ideas, but with every book he gets closer to outright rejection of modern medical thinking in favor of his own weird blend of folk medicine, superstition, and wild claims about the effects of laughter on the body."

I envisioned humor clinics staffed with Borscht Belt veterans and young comedy club interns, serving the one-liner health needs of the country. Laughter, the new Laetrile.

Pescatore went on. "Until he actually declares modern medicine his enemy, his critics are on shaky ground. That could be soon. I've heard some wild rumors about his next book, which, by the way, earned him a six-figure advance."

"I don't think it matters *what's* in his next book. Critics will still have trouble proving he's a sham."

"Speaking from experience?"

"Yes, not with Novak, but with people like him. Holding up a book on TV creates unassailable credibility. My own crusades against charlatans often accomplished little more than giving free publicity to the very humbugs I was trying to discredit."

I asked Pescatore if he knew the story of Novak's "miracle healing." The tale Pescatore told was basically the same one I had heard, except he thought the boardinghouse fire had been in Maine and that Novak had been buried in rubble for three days. He asked Benny, who said he heard that Novak was burned in a car wreck in the middle of an Arizona desert. I consulted my copy of Novak's book.

"The back cover says a boardinghouse caught fire in the Northwest. Based on the story-distortion alone, we've got a living legend on our hands, Randy."

I told him about Novak's offer to erase my smoking habit.

"Try it," he said. "It's most likely some variation on autosuggestion. It's amazing what can happen when you're in a relaxed state, focusing on a behavior goal. Sometimes the unexpected happens."

"What if it brainwashes me into joining a secret slave cult in a foreign land?

"Drop me a postcard . . . in crayon, so I know it's you."

When Mrs. Lloyd Ames of Hagerstown, Maryland, answered the phone, she thought I was her husband. He hadn't called for two weeks, but she said she wasn't worried, only annoyed. I told her I was Ames's new sales manager at Crown Laboratories.

"What was your name again?"

"Merlin." I was wearing out that name. Maybe I should have renewed my subscription to *The Alias Monthly*.

"Lloyd never said he had a new manager. What happened to Mr. Dardik?"

"Sad case. He quit to join a cult of brainwashed slaves. His resignation letter was in crayon."

"Only ten months to retirement, too. Never know, do you?"

"Does your husband often go this long without calling?"

"No, but you know the salesman's life. We've moved once a year since we married. I've taken six driver's tests. In fact, we just recently moved again. Only, this time, it was completely unexpected. When Lloyd married me, he conned me into thinking we'd plant roots in Montana."

She thanked me for calling, saying she appreciated my concern for the salesmen's families. Not like old Dardik. She said she had seen his radical religious conversion coming for years.

With the phone propped against my shoulder, I swiveled back and forth in the desk chair and eyed my jumble of notes and papers. I looked again at the phone number in the first page of Cate's résumé and dialed Mick Salny, her agent. He answered his own phone. Some agent.

I said, "Mr. Salny, I'm casting a film that shoots in September. Most locations are in Southern California. It's an ensemble piece, lots of diverse characters. We want new faces, no stars. I'm interested in one your clients. Cate Fleming."

My insides withered.

Next I called Stanley Trimble, the man who was going to launch me into trade-show stardom. My new career seemed further away by the hour. He answered his own phone, too. First ring.

I started outlining the publicity stunt I was planning, but he broke me off and told me that he was currently interviewing other magicians to fill my spot. I asked him for an advance on my wages and he said no; he had temporary cash-flow problems. He didn't mention the five-thousand-dollar windfall from Jack.

He asked if I was still snooping around in Roselle. Because my mouth still tasted bad after the last two calls, I was honest and said yes. When you're honest with people like Stanley Trimble, they either think you're speaking a foreign tongue or they get furious. Stanley did the latter. And hung up.

Further on in the introduction to Novak's book I read that his legendary boardinghouse fire had been in Billings, Montana, in 1960. I called three hospitals in Billings. One official gave me the number of a retired doctor whose last name was easy to remember.

I dialed his number. He was at home and seemed glad to talk. If I had been selling light bulbs, I could have unloaded a case. All I was peddling, though, were unpleasant, dark memories.

"Dr. Burns, you were one of the physicians that treated victims of that boardinghouse fire in 1960? Yes, you know which one I mean? The Burnette Boarding House? Have you ever heard of Lorenz Novak?"

I learned that Burns also knew Lloyd Ames, the drug salesman, and that many people died in that fire (a fact Novak never mentioned). He also said that even though Lorenz Novak had been a fire victim, no one by that name had been in that boardinghouse. I asked him to explain.

Jack entered the office, his fingers rubbing slow circles on his chest. He eyed the paperwork on the desk and said, "Do I need an appointment to use my own office?"

"I'm finished. I'm just making sure the hotel's final phone bill will be a dandy. I'll pay for the calls, of course."

"Forget it."

"Hey, you look beat. Here." I got up, and he took my seat without argument. "You weren't practicing hand-springs with the clowns, were you?"

"No. Spillman adjourned the acrobatics session soon after it started. Hodge tried matching Spillman move for move, and now he's wearing his arm in a sling. Cate did the best, even better than Novak. She knew which tricks to attempt and which to pass up."

Jack leafed through Cate's résumé, lingering over the shower photo.

"They're outside now," he said. "Want to watch?"

We went into the conference room to watch the troupe through the window. The hard-hatted demolition workers sat cross-legged on the sidewalk in front of the Edison Building. Each performer did a short routine for them. None of the contestants wore makeup, relying solely on pantomime for laughs. Cate, in a belted tunic that allowed free movement, did an improvised comic dance. She was unruffled when the tunic popped open in the middle of her gyrations. She quickly reknotted it. Her audience loved it, some whistling their approval.

One worker walked among the other spectators, taking up a collection in his upside-down metal hat. Spillman didn't stop him; the cash was a symbol of his charges' progress. The man shook Spillman's hand in gratitude.

The workers' foreman, wearing a white helmet, motioned the men back to work. Break time was over.

Sitting on a folding chair in the conference room, I spread my phone-conversation notes on my lap. Jack had gone to his room to lie down. He said he had been napping more and more lately.

I arranged and rearranged the slips of paper, feeling like a three-card-monte dealer. No fresh ideas emerged. Only the lingering images of the clowns and their worker audience.

Their hatful of money was an unwelcome reminder of my own sardonic jokes of someday taking to the streets.

Maybe I was envious. Although ragtag, the clowns were still entertainers. Whereas I was facing a future in trade shows, where a company's product, not I, would be the star.

I realized no ironclad contract bound me to Trimble. Also, I could leave the Fitch and the mire surrounding Vaughn's death anytime I chose.

Nobody had a gun to my head.

Yet.

CHAPTER EIGHTEEN

It was late evening when I entered the storage room in the basement of the Fitch. Hodge was just finishing up his cataloguing work. Before going upstairs, he gave me permission to explore his files and even gave me a computer mini-lesson. He claimed he was quitting early because of exhaustion, but I think he felt safer in his locked hotel room. He denied thinking there was a connection between his project and his being attacked.

I was reading a magic magazine's fluffy review of the 1966 Magicade Convention when Cate came down and pulled up a chair next to me.

"Working?" she said.

"Supposed to be. I was hoping I'd stumble onto a buried secret, something worth killing for, but I keep getting sidetracked. Too many memories in this room."

"Feeling nostalgic?"

"I hate that word. It implies that *old* equals *good*. . . ."

"You didn't answer my question."

I closed the magazine I was reading and walked my fingers through a box of *Linking Ring* magazines, stopping at a nine-year-old issue that featured Cate and me on the cover, clutching a ten-gallon loving cup. I couldn't recall which award it was; the engraved letters were too tiny to read. I was trim and tan, and Cate, one black-gloved hand on her hip, was all legs and cleavage in a slinky showgirl getup. She wore a frosty smile and looked unsubtly seductive.

Cate leaned close to me, giving the magazine a cursory glance. I inhaled her scent.

"Exploring all these artifacts makes me wistful, but not nostalgic," I said. "By the way, I read your résumé."

"Wonderful. When do you sign me for the three-picture deal?"

"That's your goal? Movies?"

"Yes."

"Isn't your geography off?" I asked. "It's a long subway ride to the West Coast from here."

"My agent moves slow. He doesn't want me to flash and burn out."

We'll soon see how slow he moves.

"Your agent—what's his name? Salny? What's he think of this contest?"

"He knows I'm here, but not that I'm competing."

"Do you think winning the rights to portray a male clown role will tickle him?"

"Maybe not. He overruled me when I wanted to list magician's assistant on my résumé. He said it would hurt my image. I wish now I hadn't given in."

I felt heartened until she added, "Everybody always asks what I did during that period. I got tired of explaining."

She buried our *Linking Ring* issue among the rest.

"Somebody searched my room," she said.

"Who?"

"I don't know. Not long after our performance for the workers, I went up to change. Before I put my key in the door, I heard a dresser drawer slide closed. I hurried back down the hall and hid in the stairwell. A few minutes later I heard a door open and close."

"Your door?"

"Maybe. I didn't want to be seen, so I stayed well away from the window in the stairwell door. When I got enough nerve to peek, I saw Bill Rupeka moving toward me, trying so hard to walk quietly, you'd have thought the insides of his shoes were lined with broken glass. When he spotted me, I couldn't think of a plausible reason why I'd be hiding behind the door, so I told him the truth about hearing a prowler. I gave him my key, and he checked out my room for me. No one was there. Everything, as far as I could tell, was exactly as I had left it.''

"Think it was Rupeka you heard in your room?"

"Could be. He blamed his funny walk on swollen feet from a strenuous day, but his gait was nearly normal by the time he left my room. Miraculous recovery."

"Yeah."

"He carries a gun, you know," she said. "He pulled it out of an ankle holster before he went into the room."

"I've seen it."

She took another look around at the basement archives and shuddered. "I'm going upstairs. You'll help me with my clown work again tonight?"

"I'll be finished here in an hour. Want to wait, and we'll go up together?"

She shook her head. "Too much to do. I'm working on my final routine."

"Inventing one yourself?"

"No. Spillman's requiring us to do one of Quimp's set pieces."

"Which did you pick?"

"The Milking Routine."

"Didn't everyone already do that?"

"Not everyone. Remember, that session was interrupted when you found Vaughn. I never got my turn, and I worked damn hard on that piece."

"Think the others will protest?"

"I don't care. Helping you hasn't left much time for learning a new routine. The milk sketch uses an audience volunteer, so, for practice, I need a body to help, somebody to stand there and act stupid. Can you handle that? It's easy. Think of all the years I did it for you."

Hmmm. What in the world, pray tell, was she trying to tell me?

I said, "Maybe I can help another way. How many times have you seen Quimp do the routine?"

"Twice."

"With all the films and tapes down here, there might be one with Quimp doing the Milk Routine. Why not take pointers from the master himself? If I find it, I'll bring it up, along with a machine to watch it on. Of course, if my being in your bedroom makes you uncomfortable—"

"Christ, Harry, relax! We weren't that big a deal."

Cate sorted through the box and again found the magazine with us on the cover. "I changed my mind. I *like* this picture. How about if I borrow it? I'm not nostalgic, you understand . . . just wistful. When you come up, we'll work on the routine and then we can do, uh, something else, something you're probably out of practice at. Once, for old time's sake. Okay?"

As she went up the steps, I replayed her words. They delighted me.

I scoured the film and tape bins for anything marked "Quimp," but no luck. Most were not labeled by individual performers. Hodge had begun cross-indexing the performers' names onto computer diskettes, and I found one entitled "Video Performances." Hodge had showed me only once how to use the disks in the computer, and I feared accidentally erasing his data. I put the diskette back into its file box.

Next to the file box I found an album of pictures taken at the Fitch in the years preceding the hotel's magic reputation, before Jack was the owner. Below each photo were hand-printed captions.

I never knew so many fraternal organizations had once existed. Regal robes and hats distinguished one organization from another, some with names straight out of Dungeons and Dragons. There were the familiar Knights of Columbus and the numerous Masonic organizations, but they stood side by side with the Ancient Order of the Knights of the Mystic Chain, Improved Order of Heptasophs, and United Daughters of Rechab—dinosaurs today.

TV never did kill radio or the movies, as many feared. What it killed was clubs.

One album devoted space to groups of plainly dressed, unsmiling people—revivalists from the 1950s who traveled gypsy-style, working nightly at local churches, auditoriums, and tents until a drop in the nightly collection dictated they again hit the road. They offered songs, sermons, and healing in return for the steady clink of change in collection plates. The pictures of these groups were badly faded. Even when I held them directly under the light, most of their faces were washed out.

The next photo album I picked up was cheerier. Irving Desfor, the magician-photographer, had captured the electricity of the first Magicade. There was Fred Kaps pouring buckets of salt from an invisible shaker, Milbourne Christopher floating an assistant through a hoop, and Senator Clark Crandall deadpanning his way through a blend of sight gags as outrageous as the Marx Brothers. My mind augmented the black-and-white pictures with color, applause, and words. Who needed video and movies?

The last picture in the album was of Spillman eating breakfast alone in the Fitch restaurant, glaring. He hated being photographed out of makeup.

I shut the album, regretting I couldn't drift longer, lost in a time when life's sweetest words were, "How did you do that?" and "Come on, show me that again." It had been a time when I had eaten, slept, and breathed magic, a time when I believed that confidence was something only old men lost.

I slid my chair over until I squarely faced the newest member of the American family.

"Just how smart are you?" I asked Hodge's computer.

I ran my fingers underneath and found the ON switch. I pushed buttons and keys until whatever I typed registered on-screen. Prior to today, my closest contact with computers had been using my pocket calculator to figure out how many of my checks were going to bounce.

I typed:

PERRY VAUGHN - DEAD.

REPUTATION - TROUBLEMAKER.

SHERIFF & M.E. SAY HE SMOTHERED DURING BURGLARY.

BUT VAUGHN WORE QUIMP MAKEUP.

QUIMP AND CLOWN CONTESTANTS DIDN'T KNOW HIM.

NOTHING REPORTED STOLEN FROM FITCH.

SHERIFF WANTS ME TO STOP ASKING QUESTIONS.

HODGE IS HURT. WHAT IS HE REALLY CATALOGUING?

JAMES LOY - LLOYD AMES, PHARMACEUTICAL SALESMAN. LIVING IN FITCH SINCE IT CLOSED. DRUGS INVOLVED?

WAS SPILLMAN THE ORIGINAL TARGET OF KILLER?

WHY WAS RUPEKA IN CATE'S ROOM?

WHY DOES NOVAK WANT TO BE QUIMP? WHY DID SPILLMAN MAKE HIM A FINALIST?

WHY? WHY? WHY? WHY?

Feeling the fool, I hit the ENTER button. My words vanished from the screen, replaced by:

ERROR   ERROR   ERROR

The blinking message mocked my computer illiteracy. What did I expect? That the machine, after mulling over all the factors, would print out the murderer's name? No, the computer had done what I had expected: it told me I was full of ERROR.

As I reached to turn the computer off, an arm wrapped around my neck and tried to crush my windpipe. My chair tilted back. Off-balance, all I could do was grope in the air for my attacker. With his other hand, he flashed a pistol in my face.

At the sight of the gun I stopped struggling, and he immediately took the death edge off his stranglehold. I hadn't seen the gun clearly enough to tell if it was Rupeka's. Or Tarrant's. I knew it wasn't Quimp's, whose gun would have unfurled a "Bang" banner. I tried to see my assailant's reflection in the computer screen. Too dark.

Your move, I thought.

Ouch. His move hurt. He pushed his gun barrel to my temple. Every time I tried to talk, he jabbed in admonition. I relented and sat still, hoping he had a calm trigger finger.

Where had he come from? Had he been hiding behind one of the shelves? Had he sneaked down the stairs? Was he a crazed magic groupie who had stalked me for weeks and was now going to show his devotion by blowing my brains out? I'd never find out unless I asked.

"Hey, are you—" He again enforced his No Talking rule with a poke of his gun. Talk about strict! How the hell was I supposed to rattle him with insouciant wisecracks if I wasn't allowed to talk?

He released his grip on my neck, flipped open a plastic door on the computer, and slid in a black envelope with a hole in the middle—a computer diskette.

He tapped a sequence of buttons. The computer ran through a series of whistles, thumps, and whirrs. Then a message came to the screen:

LET'S PLAY KIDNAP!

He hit ENTER. Then:

HOWDY HARRY!!!! WANNA PLAY?
(KINDLY PRESS ENTER AFTER EACH
MESSAGE)

At the urging of his gun, I hit ENTER.

NO TALKING.
DON'T RESIST.
GAME IMMEDIATELY ENDS IF YOU ATTEMPT
TO ESCAPE.

I hit ENTER without any more prompting. I was getting good at this game.

FOLLOW THE CUES OF YOUR CAPTOR.
AND GOOD LUCK!!!!!!!!

I hit ENTER again, and a crude top hat appeared on the screen. An animated rabbit popped up and waved a sad goodbye to me.

My captor tied a black cloth over my eyes, pulling it as tight as a tourniquet. He did the same with a gag over my mouth. His next "cue" was to grab me by the throat and jerk me out of the chair.

KIDNAP was a misnomer. MURDER was the name of this game, and I bet there wasn't a YOU WIN, HARRY!!!! message programmed anywhere on that disk.

He led me to the center of the room and clubbed me across the side of the head with his gun butt. I dipped to my knees. I never fully lost consciousness and was vaguely aware of what was happening. He bound my hands behind me with something strong and thin, probably fishing line. As he pulled me to my feet, I felt off-balance, as though standing on a moving bus.

I heard something roll across the floor. He nudged me forward, and I almost tripped. Prodded again, I stepped up on a ledge. It moved back and forth. A cart, probably used to transport luggage in and out of the hotel. My kidnapper dropped a body-length canvas bag over me and forced me to lie down. He pushed my feet inside the bag and drew the ends tight. Every time I moved, he prodded me with his foot.

He pushed the cart out of the storage room and down the hall, bouncing over the wide cracks in the cement floor.

We stopped, and I heard him walk back to the computer. The snapping sound told me that he had remembered to remove his disk from the computer. He turned the machine off with a click. Damn.

Returning, he pushed me along until we got to the top of an incline so steep I nearly rolled off the cart. My captor raised the big metal door at the other end of the basement, and the far-off sounds of the garment factory filtered through the bag.

He wheeled me out of the Fitch as if I were a sack of five-o'clock mail.

Our journey was bumpy but short, lasting less than a block. When the cart halted, we were inside another building. He rolled me off the cart. Although the building shielded me from the wind, the place was unheated. I braced myself for the click of his pistol hammer, but all I heard were his diminishing footsteps and the squeak of the cart's wheels as he pushed it along. Shortly, his footsteps were out on the sidewalk, blending into the distant clanking of the factory's night shift.

I tried escaping from my cocoon—and learned how smart my captor was. He hadn't tied the bag shut with more string, but with wire, probably repeatedly twisting the ends with a pliers. I soon tired of rolling and struggling. Through the bag, the uncarpeted floor felt gritty.

As the hours passed, I tried different strategies. Numb, my bound hands felt around the bag, searching for a worn spot that might yield to added stress. I positioned myself so that I could bang the wire through the cloth with my head. My forehead bled, but the wire wouldn't weaken.

I made slow progress in working the gag free, even trying to bite my way through. All I got was a mouth that tasted like a cotton lollipop. I was, however, able to slide the blindfold loose.

My spirits rose as more time passed without the return of the kidnapper. I could tell dawn had arrived because there was murky brown through the canvas where every-thing had previously been black. When I heard the banter of nearby workers reporting for work, I realized where I was. And why.

Only one more building left to be torn down.

I was inside the Edison, and I was supposed to be its last tenant.

How were they going to destroy the building? Piece by piece? If so, then the workers would find themselves a sack containing one worn-out but alive magician. But explosives would most likely be their pry bar and wrecking ball today. The kidnapper intended the workers to find pieces of canvas, along with scraps of bone and flesh.

Again I tried wriggling and rolling, managing three revolutions. Because my hands were still securely bound, I couldn't take my weight off the parts of my body that ached. My fingers felt broken. By rubbing the side of my face repeatedly against the floor, I finally worked my gag loose.

Then I heard footsteps outside.

Heavy, not stealthy.

Now inside the building and getting closer.

The sonofabitch was making sure he did the job right.

I stopped trying to roll, and my position went fetal.

Not the click, please. I didn't want to hear that click of his pistol's hammer.

I know there's no such thing as mind reading, but he must have read mine.

Click.

I stiffened, waiting for the gun's explosion. Nothing.

In my mind I listened again to the click and realized that it wasn't a gun hammer I had heard, but a ballpoint pen.

I knew now who it was.

Jeffers.

I wanted to kiss him right through the canvas bag.

CHAPTER NINETEEN

"Jeffers. Let me out. What the hell you waiting for?"

Another click, and he put his pen away. This made the fifth year in a row I had heard that same click.

"Harry?"

"I'm in the bag."

"Where? My eyes aren't used to the dark in here yet."

"If you think it's dark out there, try this bag."

"Keep talking. I'll zero in on your voice. That's it. Keep going."

I babbled nonstop, even after Jeffers found me. It was nonsense stream of consciousness, mostly about how much I hated his guts and how much I hated losing.

With his finger he poked my ribs through the bag and giggled. I recovered sufficiently to say, "What's so funny?"

"I was wondering what you'd do if you found me in a similar predicament."

"I'd perform my patriotic duty. I'd paste stamps on the bag and mail you to Alaska."

He clucked his tongue. "But you expect *me* to play Sir Galahad?"

"Certainly. You fancy yourself as a white knight, don't you?"

"Harry, I'm just a working stiff who serves the public."

"Yeah. The same way Bela Lugosi's character served the public."

"It was that bad a year for you, eh?"

I didn't know if he heard me sigh through the canvas.

"You'll be out in a minute," he said.

But I wasn't.

"Wow, this wire's braided tight," he said. "I ripped up my fingers trying to untwist it. Can't break it, either."

"You don't carry wire cutters? I thought they'd be standard issue, along with armor-piercing bazookas."

"You're supposed to be the hotshot escapist: The Man Who Walks Through Walls."

"That was Houdini's billing. I tell you, whoever bagged me knew his stuff. Even Houdini couldn't escape from this."

I heard him start to walk away.

"Hey, where are you going?"

"To find those construction guys. They were all down the block when I came in the back way. They'll lend me cutters."

"The back way? Wait. They don't know you're in here?"

"No."

"Dammit, forget the cutters, Jeffers. Just get us out of here."

He sensed my fear and didn't ask questions.

There was a jerk, and the floor slid beneath me. I scrambled within the bag to find a position that didn't hurt. Friction heated the bag's bottom. Litter and debris gouged me as Jeffers dragged me along on a rough, speedy ride.

Outside, sidewalk cracks regularly jarred me. Then we stopped. I yelled to keep going, but his answer was obscured by his dog-like panting. Starting again, he pulled me off the curb, and I bounced onto the street, upping my bruise count.

The pace nearly doubled. Someone was helping him. I heard distant men's voices shouting advice, sounding like ringside boxing spectators.

When we halted again, Jeffers said to his helper, "Got any cutters?" They dropped the end of the sack, and my ankles smacked the pavement. Journey's end. I stretched out, waiting to be released. Every escape artist's nightmare: somebody else freeing him.

In a few minutes I heard ripping noises and breathed fresh air. A knife was slitting my bag. I squinted at the light, dodging the blade each time it plunged.

When I emerged from the bag, I tried to look dignified. *Hey, folks, no problem. Just a routine kidnapping and attempted murder.*

We were in front of the Fitch. Jeffers sat on the curb, head between his legs as sweat ran to the ends of his hair and dribbled to the ground. A man wearing a hard hat and smelling of snuff made careful sawing motions with his penknife, freeing my hands. I recognized him as the one who loaned me the truck the other day.

"Must have been one *hell* of a bill you forgot to pay this time," he said. "We delayed the blast when we saw both you coming. Pretty close, though."

Under the pretense of brushing dust off my clothes, I coaxed back my circulation.

Jeffers pointed and said, "Cops are here already. Quick, weren't they?"

Sheriff Tarrant and Deputy Wirfel stood on the sidewalk. They both acknowledged me with glances, but resumed their distant, trance-like stares. I turned to see what was the object of their fascination. Ah, the Edison Building, my would-be crypt.

Standing with the two lawmen were all the current hotel residents—except Cate. Put a height scale behind them, and I'd have had my own personal lineup. I didn't even need a two-way mirror to observe without being observed. Everyone was too intent on not missing the spectacle of the Edison going down like the proverbial house of cards. As I walked down the lineup, each head tilted to look around me.

"Close call?" Tarrant said, eyes straight ahead.

"No thanks to you."

"The deputy and I are here this morning to provide security. When they demolish buildings, it sometimes draws strange elements. I was unaware of your plight, you understand.''

"And if you had known?"

"I'd have pushed the detonator myself. Ten minutes ago."

"Where were you two-thirty this morning?"

"Same place you were."

I looked inquisitive.

He gave a horse laugh and said, "In the sack."

I moved on to Wirfel, who said, "Don't believe him. The sheriff would have rescued you. You don't know him like I do."

"I didn't see *you* roll out the Welcome Wagon when I got desacked either, Deputy."

I asked him where he was at two-thirty.

"With my wife. We were doing our income taxes. Yeah, I know it's the last minute."

I did a tsk-tsk and moved on to Jack.

"This is it," he said. "Next they'll be wiring dynamite to the old Fitch."

"I hate to ask, Jack, but do you have a two-thirty alibi?"

His expression told me that one more such question would endanger our friendship. He shook his head no, with eyes fixed on the doomed building.

Next was Hodge. I skipped him. Playing computer and keeping the gun on me took two good hands, and Hodge had hurt himself during Quimp's acrobatics yesterday. No man with his arm in a sling could have bound and gagged me and then carted me down the block.

He said, "Welcome to the club. I hope you find out who did this." As I passed, I bumped his arm hard, and he jumped. His pain was real and unrehearsed. I felt guilty, but I had to know.

Novak, standing next to Hodge, said, "Almost lost you, didn't we?"

I looked at the magazine under his arm. It was the one with Cate and me on the cover.

"After you disappeared, Cate couldn't sleep," Novak

explained. "She knocked on my door, and we went downstairs to look for you. She was carrying this magazine at the time and consented to lend it to me. You gave us a scare."

"Gave myself one, too."

"I liked your interview." He tapped the magazine. "It gave me insight into your theories on entertainment. But your views on the paranormal disturb me. Don't you believe in *any* extra-scientific explanation of mysterious phenomena?"

"Nope."

"But surely your rescue today is a miracle. How did that man find you? Telepathy?"

"No. Jeffers is no deity, although sometimes he thinks he is. There was no mind reading, more like mind memorization. Jeffers knows quite well the way I think."

"You have a narrow mind, Mr. Colderwood."

"Thanks for the compliment. Just think how narrow a razor's edge is. You're upset because in that interview I did everything but call your type a fraud. Old article, though. Today I *would* call you a fraud."

Novak's face flushed in anger. When I asked him for his alibi, he thrust a business card in my hand. It was his agent's. "He's also my lawyer, and releases all my statements on legal matters." He again regarded the Edison. "You know, it's fascinating how they demolish these old buildings. They strategically plant explosives to direct the blast in precisely the direction they want. The building really blows *in*, not *up*. An implosion."

"Glad you're well versed on the subject," I said.

With one sidestep, I now faced Rupeka, who looked guilty. He stared at his shoes, my shoes, the sidewalk, the sky—everything but me and the Edison Building. He was unshaven.

"Got up in a hurry today, Bill?" I said.

He touched his fingers to his coarse face. "Slept in. I've been working on my final routine. Maybe I should ease up."

"Good idea. Maybe you didn't sleep at all last night. Must have really dressed fast, since your socks don't match."

He nearly fell for it, almost lifting up his pant legs. I wanted to compare the gun in his ankle holster with my memory of the kidnapper's gun. I asked for his alibi.

"Go to hell," he said.

"What were you doing in Cate Fleming's room last night?"

"Helping her flush out a possible prowler."

"Impossible task if you *were* the prowler."

"Mrs. Fleming was, and still is, too good for you, Colderwood."

I regurgitated his previous three-word travel suggestion and reminded him that Cate was a married woman.

I turned my back on the building that had such hypnotic attraction for the others and walked toward the hotel entrance. Jeffers followed.

As I entered the lobby, Cate stood up. Her eyes were a glistening red. I couldn't tell if it was from tears or lack of sleep. We hugged each other. Her embrace was not romantic, but one of relief. Jeffers stood at the opposite side of the lobby.

"I told Sheriff Tarrant you were missing," she said, "but he said there wasn't much he could do until forty-eight hours elapsed."

"After forty-eight hours he'd have found other excuses."

"I couldn't go out to watch that building blow up. I'd have felt like a vulture."

I told her about my abduction and Jeffers's rescue. She said, "He's the guy you've been running from the last few days?"

"His name is Duane Jeffers. I met him the same year you left. I've never known a more relentless bastard. If he were a reporter, he'd have made Woodward and Bernstein look lazy. But he loves his current job, and I'm stuck with him. Probably forever."

"What does he do?"

"He's a government employee for an obscure department called the Internal Revenue Service."

"Are you in tax trouble, Harry?"

"Just the opposite. Everything's all square. Jeffers sees to it. He's a field agent, specializing in tracking down hard-to-find citizens and serving them with audit notices. When he was assigned to me five years ago, I avoided him every way I knew. When he finally cornered me, he told me no one had ever eluded him so long. That's when he made the wager: he bet I couldn't hide from him for more than seven days once he started looking for me."

"Good thing you're a magician."

"It doesn't help against him. He's an amateur magician himself."

"How much do you wager?"

"Same every year—my total federal tax tally."

"He must be a powerful man to pull enough strings to exempt you from taxes."

"Oh, he can't keep me from being taxed. If he can't find me in seven days, he pays my taxes out his own pocket . . . for the next five years. The stakes have dwindled annually because my income's been on a slide, but I hope the year I finally beat him is the year I'm back on top."

"Doesn't he catch hell for devoting so much time to just one case?"

"He doesn't use work time; he takes a week's vacation to play our manhunt game. He says it's relaxing. I don't feel singled out, either. The kind of deductions I take cinches that I'll be audited every year anyway."

"He must think he's good."

"He *is* good."

Jeffers walked over and unceremoniously pulled out a pen and a sheaf of papers. "Harry's getting better," he said to Cate. "Every year he gives me less and less vacation to enjoy after serving him notice."

He handed me the papers that announced the place and

time to bring my books for auditing. I signed the two copies and handed one back to him.

He checked my signature, pocketed his copy, and said,
"Perhaps you'll beat me by the turn of the century."

"How'd you find me?" I asked.

"I didn't see you being abducted, since I was upstairs
paying a visit to Cate."

"You were?" she said. "Oh, wait. You were the flo-
rist?"

He nodded and asked her how many florists deliver at
that hour.

"I thought the flowers were from—from someone I
knew." She looked so hurt, I wished I had sent them.

"Flowers open doors," Jeffers said, as if he were quot-
ing one of Newton's laws of motion. "I asked Cate where
you were, letting her think that I needed you to settle up
the flower bill. She said she had last seen you in the basement. When I checked down there, the computer was still
warm. Later on I mentioned to Hodge about the computer,
and he showed me how the special circuitry can restore
data that had been in the computer before it was turned off.
What we found was a dreadful game called Kidnap. Really
primitive graphics."

"Hodge told me a friend of his put in that special circuitry," I said.

"I was sure it wasn't a joke. It was too ghoulish, even
for you, Harry. As soon as I learned that that office building down the block was to be detonated, I rushed over to
check it out. I had no idea they were going to level it so
soon." He looked at his watch. "I have a little time, do
you think that we could . . . ?" He made a shuffling motion with his hands.

It was the same ritual every year. For twenty minutes
we all sat on the lobby sofa as Jeffers demonstrated his
latest close-up magic. For his first trick, he spirited a
marked card into a sealed box that Cate held in her hand
the whole time. Then he did a cups-and-balls routine with
sponge chickens appearing under the cups as the finale.

Almost as an afterthought, he plucked gold coins from each chicken. I wondered if this symbolism was accidental. Having an insatiable desire to improve his magic, he constantly prodded me for constructive criticism. We swapped news of the magic world—who was performing where, convention news, and the latest tricks on the market. I didn't keep up with the magic magazines anymore.

When finished, he stood up and said, "Well, I got a plane to catch. I'll be spending the rest of my vacation in Vegas, testing a new blackjack system."

"Of course, you pay taxes on all your winnings, right?" Cate asked.

"That goes without saying," Jeffers said. He smiled at Cate and wished her luck in the clown competition.

After he left she said, "Harry, you didn't even say thank you. He saved your life."

"That would have been an insult. He was just doing his job. Dead men can't pay taxes. With me gone, what would Jeffers do for fun on his vacation?"

The table in front of us vibrated and slid sideways a half inch. The roar from the Edison Office Building rose slowly and lasted several seconds.

I saw that Jeffers had forgotten his sponge chickens. They did a twitching dance to the edge of the table and toppled off.

CHAPTER TWENTY

I wanted to deaden my body aches with a hot shower, but I lacked the ambition to drag myself upstairs to—what was my new room number?—oh, yes, 636. I had almost forgotten. No giant key tag to remind me. Maybe I should fasten one to my lock pick.

I moved around in the lobby chair until my throbbing dropped to just below pain level. If Novak were here, he would have smooth-talked my hurt away with mental suggestions seasoned with witty anecdotes. I imagined my bruises magically healing before my eyes, like Hyde turning into Jekyll.

I reached for the newspaper on the table beside me. The *Roselle Sun* shone only three days a week. This was yesterday's edition, with late-breaking scoops on Rotary meetings, lost pets, and town-council squabbles.

Ordinarily I'd turn straight to the entertainment page. Today I gave the police blotter top priority. The Roselle crime beat made brief reading. The K-Mart bagged a half-dozen shoplifters. One drunk driver smacked into another drunk driver at three A.M.—no injuries from the wreck, although both sustained multiple contusions from their fist-fight. There was an attempted grocery-store burglary—no one apprehended. Also, an unidentified man, hauled in for drunkenness, subdued a sheriff's deputy and escaped. The article didn't mention that the drunk had also done some clandestine photocopying.

Cate offered to give me a massage, but a news story

about a crime in another town dictated otherwise. Upon reading it I knew I'd be journeying to the county just south of Roselle. First, I needed more cardboard credibility. My Society of American Magicians membership card was not the greatest door-opener.

Rupeka solved my problem. When he entered the lobby, I stood up and took a roundhouse swing at him. He blocked it, giving me a quick karate kick to the kidneys and a knee to the chin. I went down like the Edison, muttering that no damn cop was going to get away with what he'd said earlier about Cate and me.

He and Cate pulled me to my feet. He apologized and said he hoped he hadn't done me damage.

"I should be the one apologizing," I said. "I don't know what the hell got into me."

They helped me up to Cate's room, where I stretched out on her bed. When Rupeka left, he reminded Cate that the morning's clown session would begin shortly.

Even though she saw through my ruse in picking the fight, Cate made good her massage offer. Where her technique was ineffective, I demonstrated the proper method, using her as a subject. She was a quick study, topping each of my lessons with embellishments of her own. Undressed, we traded secrets at an increasingly furious pace. Needless to say, she was late for Quimp's session.

Later, out in the hall, I saw that Rupeka had hung a Don't Disturb sign on the door. He had seen through my act, too. Although not completely.

I hoped in the next few hours he wouldn't need his Visa card, or anything else from his wallet.

"Sorry, restricted area. Criminal investigation in progress."

I handed the policeman my ID. He studied it. "Sorry, Officer Rupeka. Is there something I can do for you?"

"The name's *Roo-pee-ka*, not *Rah-peck-a*, and I'm not here on business. Just passing through on vacation. Need a hand?"

He looked up the road toward my van, conveniently parked far enough away to hide its dents and scraped paint. He seemed satisfied with the ID and was willing to trade courtesies with an out-of-state cop. He flopped shut the wallet but held on to it.

"You don't pick up hitchhikers as a habit, do you?" he said.

I laughed at the question, and said, "I see enough tragic results of Good Samaritanism during my working hours."

"For the next twenty miles, if you see anyone thumbing, stop at a phone and give our office a buzz."

"So this is the hitchhiker case I read about in the *Roselle Sun?*"

He nodded.

"How many murders does this make? Three?"

"No. Four."

"Same MO for this one?"

"Almost. This victim's been dead only two days. The others took longer to discover."

The brush swished behind him, and another man in uniform tromped up the embankment to road level. He sat down on the bumper of their squad car and caught his breath while picking briars out of his uniform.

The first cop introduced me by simply showing him the wallet.

"Find anything?" the first cop asked.

"Not a stitch," the other said.

I said, "You're looking for clothing. Right?"

"Yes and no," the first said. "We theorize the murderer's a hitchhiker. In the other cases, the victims' vehicles were recovered several miles away, abandoned and banged up. This stretch of road has become the killer's body dump. We can do without that kind of litter. Like the first three, this body was nude. Near each of the sites, we found a T-shirt and a pair of jeans. The discarded clothing has always been the same size."

"The hitchhiker discards his own clothes and wears the victims'? Why?" I said.

"Damned if I know," the partner said. The car bumper dipped as he pushed himself to his feet.

Their radio squawked a string of numbers and letters. The two nodded knowingly, so I nodded along with them, figuring the real Rupeka would know all that cop code. The first officer took his time getting into the car to answer the call.

I had jotted down my questions before leaving the Fitch. I now hoped the first policeman, distracted by his partner's radio conversation, wouldn't listen critically to these questions.

"Is the autopsy complete on this latest victim?"

"We're still waiting."

"No ID?"

"None."

"Is your coroner a forensic pathologist?"

He started to open the wallet. "Where'd you say you were from?"

"I thought this was Ted Crowell's county."

"You're one county off, Rupeka. The famous M.E. lives up in Roselle. Our autopsy is being performed at the Adair Medical Center."

"Why doesn't your county employ Crowell as a consultant? How busy could he be?"

"We prefer things our way."

"So Dr. Crowell still has his, uh, problem?" I said, launching my fishing expedition. I reeled in a whopper on my first try.

He said, "I hear the county officials up there made sure no loose funds were in their coroner's office for Crowell to dip into. Still, depending on how you look at it, it's good for all. Crowell's grateful to practice his profession again, and his community feels lucky to have his services. As for *this* county, we'll gladly pay out the money for the important postmortems and know that no one's hocking microscopes on the side."

I tried for more fish, but didn't get a nibble. He was

noncommittal about Sheriff Tarrant's reputation. He claimed relative ignorance about the Perry Vaughn case.

I wanted to leave, but he still hadn't returned the wallet. I reached for it. He opened it again. "Old wallet, Officer Rupeka?"

Oh, boy. The fish were now casting lines back at me. "Yeah."

"Thought so. This ID of yours isn't current. It expired two months ago. You should toss it out."

I reached for it, and he jerked it back a few inches before I could grasp it. I had images of him and his partner playing catch while I tried to intercept it. He grinned, showing his good-natured teasing, and gave me back the wallet.

I pocketed it. Within an hour it would be back in Rupeka's room.

His partner signed off the radio and got out of the car. "Autopsy's done. Same MO again," he said, joining us. "The medical report indicates stabbing, just like the first three."

"ID him?" I said.

"Not yet. We'll trace back all abandoned cars that are discovered. That'll probably be our breaking lead."

I walked back to my van, wondering what kind of market there was for stolen microscopes.

CHAPTER TWENTY-ONE

As I walked down the hall, I could hear Spillman in his room, still dropping his coin, though not so often as before. Sometimes it would roll and he would chase after it, stumbling into furniture.

I walked up the hall to Rupeka's room and knocked on the door. I listened to Spillman drop his coin one more time, then knocked again. No answer, so I let myself in. With the door closed behind me, I could still faintly hear Spillman practicing.

I chucked Rupeka's wallet under his bed, just out of sight. When he found it, there was a chance he'd think he simply had dropped it there. Not willing to risk a full search, I took a quick survey of the room. It looked as if the maids had just cleaned it, only all the maids were gone from the Fitch. On the dresser was his copy of Quimp's book, *Clowning and Living*.

An envelope marked his place at the beginning of the chapter "The Buffoon as Political Scapegoat." The return address on the envelope was a post-office box in Boston.

Having promised myself not to stay longer than five drops of Spillman's coin, I was now pushing my luck. Spillman was working on number seven. I replaced the envelope and left. It was time to pay a visit to a political scapegoat.

Spillman wore a navy crewneck sweater that revealed an inch of white shirt collar underneath, making him look like a clergyman. Pinned to his chest was a button the size of a jar lid, depicting in fluorescent colors a sickeningly cheerful clown's head. Spillman invited me to touch its nose. I did, and it blinked on and off, emitting a shrill electronic laugh. A neon jester.

"Nice, huh?" he said, dropping his practice coin. I retrieved it from under my chair.

"This button was a gift from a former student of Otto Griebling."

Griebling was a clown acclaimed by peers but who never became a household name like Emmett Kelly.

I returned his half-dollar, and he plunged ahead with his sleight of hand. With the tip of his tongue poking out the corner of his mouth, he studied his manipulations in the dresser mirror. Within days, Spillman had advanced from the infant to the toddler stage. He now dropped or flashed the coin only once every ten attempts. All thumbs before, he was now, say, six and a half thumbs.

"Someone coached you?" I asked.

He nodded, which broke his concentration. I again played fetch.

"Who? Rupeka?"

"No. Novak gave me the pointers, but I need more."

I had learned early in life that men who wear electric clown badges do not give subtle hints. I pointed out to him a few critical ways to improve his technique, then sat back and, for the next half hour, watched that same coin disappear again and again. Sometimes it vanished without a trace. Other times it remained highly visible, rolling under the dresser or bouncing off his shoe. He took all my suggestions, but he ignored all my questions about the clown competitors.

When I left, Spillman was down to being four and three-quarters thumbs, and I was left wondering if Novak knew more magic than he was letting on.

Sitting cross-legged in Room 636, I opened my copy of *Laughter, the Healthy O.D.*

The heading on the last page was "About the Author." Yes, indeed. What about the author?

The slim summary of Novak's life was barely disguised advertisement for his previous books. It listed his television appearances and honorary college degrees. His main claim to medical authority was his recovery from "life-threatening injuries."

I turned to the preface and again read about that Montana boardinghouse fire. Doctors had given up on him. On his deathbed, barely conscious, Novak formulated Giggle Therapy. Using it, he had tittered himself back to health, wealth, and bookstore autograph parties. He wrote in the introduction, "They thought I was either insane or a miracle. I am neither."

That wasn't the story that Dr. Burns of Billings, Montana, had told me.

So what *are* you, Novak?

I intended to find out.

Like fallen autumn leaves, my notes on the Vaughn case had multiplied exponentially, carpeting my room. I taped the paper scraps to the wall, hoping that surrounding myself with all these scribbled facts and impressions would inspire me to see things anew. Instead I imagined myself cramming for a final test after attending only half the classes.

Someone knocked on the door—three fast and four slow. It was either Cate or an old college chum using our fraternity's secret knock.

It was Cate.

"I love your interior decorator," she said, looking at my "bulletin board."

"This is what my brain looks like, sliced thin and taped to the wall."

She strolled along my collection of notes as though it were an art exhibit. "Ted Crowell, the medical examiner, has a tainted past?" she said when she got to the most recent slips.

"I'm going to find out."

"I see you're also going to check out Rupeka's background, too. Do you think he attacked Hodge?"

"Maybe. Somebody doesn't like Hodge's basement research. What's he getting close to? Am I getting close to the same thing? Hodge's assailant was probably the same one that tried to blow me up."

"Any theories yet why Vaughn was dressed as Quimp?"

"None. It's hard enough to understand why all you contestants want to dress as Quimp."

Preoccupied with one of my notes, she didn't answer. She peeled it off the wall. I peeked over her shoulder, and flushed when I saw it. I didn't think I'd posted any of *those*. I tried snatching it, but she jerked away. After rereading the note, she gazed at me, eyes wide with surprise.

"You never *once* told me you felt this way," she said, folding the paper twice and slipping it into her pocket. "You've hardly ever showed me."

I slid my fingertip under one of her shoulder straps. It drifted off her shoulder. The wind outside picked up, and a draft seeped into the room, flapping the slips of paper against the wall.

I proceeded to show her exactly how I felt. Well, almost. I did my best to conceal my guilt over my phone call to her agent. I'd be calling him again soon.

Cate straightened her clothing in the mirror, then she walked to the window. "There's Novak. Looks worried, doesn't he?" she said.

"Downright panicked, I'd say."

Novak slammed the door of his Mark IV and moved like a chased rabbit, head pivoting at every sound. He scurried toward the hotel entrance, only to retreat to his car. I thought he might get in and drive away, but he changed his mind yet again. This time, keeping sharp watch, he returned, entering the hotel.

Cate got my binoculars.

"He's inside," I said, but I saw that she was focusing the binoculars on his car.

"Here," she said, handing me them.

"Hey, nice car. Maybe he'll swap pink slips for my van."

"Look at his windshield."

"Yeah, I see. Come summer, his air conditioner's going to work overtime."

On the driver's side, the windshield had a hole the size of a nickel.

"I'm going to check out that windshield," she said.

"We'd better get your practice in first."

"Okay."

She started through her final Quimp routine. When it came time for the milk to vanish, she crushed the paper cone too soon, thus diminishing the shock element. On the third try, she got it perfect. Then Cate "pierced" her elbow with an ice pick, while I played the part of the audience volunteer who held the funnel for the stream of milk that flowed out.

At the trick's climax, she poured out a flood of gumballs from an "empty" miniature milk can. She ran through the ending only once because it took so long to gather the gumballs.

When she finished, she helped me rehearse the stunt I was planning.

We tried making love again, but succeeded only in proving that I wasn't the magic man I thought. When I told her so, she laughed, and for the first time, I spoke the words written on the slip of paper in her pocket.

After she left, I spent fifteen minutes trying to think of any reasons why I shouldn't just gas up the van, call Phil Fleming to say I was stealing back his wife, and then head out on the road with Cate . . . in the opposite direction of Allentown. Instead, I laid out my list of phone numbers and started dialing.

The operator at Resnick and Mal Publishers connected

me with the publicity department, and I identified myself
as a reporter doing a story on Lorenz Novak for a Sunday
supplement.

I said, "I've already interviewed Novak, and I need to
verify some facts. Novak mentioned some trouble with his
upcoming book. Will it be published as planned?"

"We will have a new Novak book out before Christmas,
but none of it will be original. It will consist of sections
reprinted from previous books."

"What exactly went wrong? Surely Novak, the preacher
of mind power, didn't get writer's block, did he?"

"No. He lost nearly ninety percent of his current manuscript."

"Lost?"

"*Zapped* is a more accurate word.

"Hello. Weirton Police Department."

Again I used the reporter ploy. "We're doing a series
on policemen with unusual side interests. I need background information on Officer William Rupeka, the magician clown."

"One moment, please."

While I was on hold, instead of the usual easy-listening
music, they played messages from McGruff, the Crime
Prevention Dog. "Sir," the receptionist said when she
came back on, "Mr. Rupeka is no longer with the force.
Would you hold again? My superior wants a word with
you."

And I wanted a word with him. While I held, McGruff
explained ways to avoid midnight burglary. He gave no
advice on repairing bullet holes in Mark IV windshields.

Next, I phoned Mick Salny, Cate's agent. He wasn't
pleased to hear from me. "That movie role's still available," I said.

There was a pause. All I heard was line static and the
sound of Salny drumming his fingers.

"Unfortunately, my client isn't available. She's committed to another project."

After several back and forths, I concluded he wasn't just bluffing to jack up contract terms. After he tried to recommend other clients of his, I expressed disappointment and wished Cate and him good luck on their current endeavor, which, I added, must be gold-lined to be bigger than the movies.

Cate needed McGruff's advice. She had just become a victim of midnight burglary.

My next call was to the U.S. Postal Service in Boston to ask who was renting the box that was the return address on the envelope in Rupeka's room. The clerk I talked to said it was the Fleming Exer-Quipment Company.

I then called Dr. Ted Crowell, identifying myself as a witness to the hit-and-run death of Dorinda Bradley. He gasped, and I hung up.

"Think I can quit?" I said.

The newspaper in Novak's hand snapped and rustled. He hadn't heard me approach.

"Pardon?" he said.

"You said you have a sure-fire method for quitting cigarettes."

Rather than paying attention to me, he seemed intent on shutting down whatever machinery of worry was cranking inside his head. The drawn look dissolved from his face along with the lines at the corners of his eyes. His shoulders went from slumped to erect. He breathed deep, and switched his Central Control from Friendly Smile to Patronizing Smile.

"Nothing's sure-fire, but I've put together a video-cassette series on goal-setting and habit-breaking. The price tag is well over a thousand, but it's inexpensive to rent."

"How about just the one on smoking?"

"I hate to break up the set, but I'll mail you—"

"I'm in a hurry. Do you have the sound track on cassette?"

"Yes."

"Could I borrow it?"

Through the lobby doors I saw Cate snooping around Novak's car. Every time Novak looked in her direction, I drifted over to block his view.

"What room are you in now?" he said.

I wouldn't tell him, so he promised to give the tape to Cate.

"Fine," I said.

By now Novak had successfully stifled every sign of stress except the sheen of sweat on his forehead. He took a sip of the ice water on the table beside him and breathed slower and deeper.

He perked up and said, "Boy, I saw a heck of an accident about six miles outside town today. Around one o'clock. You didn't happen to drive past, did you?"

"My God, Novak. Are you trying to check *me* for an alibi?"

He denied it, but his shoulders were sloped again. The crow's-feet returned to his eyes, and his forehead was once again bathed in sweat.

Before leaving him to his internal battles, I held out my pack of Luckies and said, "Cigarette?"

He refused, looking insulted. And tense. Very tense.

CHAPTER TWENTY-TWO

Some people realize it the first time they comb their hair differently and notice all that hidden gray. Or maybe the first time they have to tilt their glasses to read distant billboards. For others it's the realization that they can no longer sit through Johnny's monologue without falling asleep. For me, the signpost of passing time was my frantic struggle to squeeze into my sequined jumpsuit—my Elvis costume. It had been months since I'd last worn it. After fastening all the snaps, buttons, zippers, I felt like a walking tourniquet. I couldn't find a painless way of crossing Cate's room. She said that my walk *was* like Elvis's . . . circa 1976. I took off the suit, vowing to lose the dozen or so pounds that had sabotaged me.

I changed into my crushed velvet tux, replete with satin stripes on the legs. I felt rinky-dink. A Holiday Inn warm-up act. But as the main attraction at the Roselle post office, it was perfect.

With its high ceilings and marble floor, the post office reminded me of an old train station. Every word spoken above a whisper echoed. A monochrome mural wrapped around three walls, depicting sweaty, smiling men in rolled-up sleeves slamming hammers onto anvils.

The people entering the building gave me wide berth, and I didn't blame them. Near midnight, post offices don't normally attract the most solid citizens. In my tux, I definitely looked unsolid. The wall clock said eleven-thirty.

"What time are they coming?" Cate asked.

"They're already late," I said, adjusting my bow tie in the stamp machine's glass.

A man shoved a parcel across the long lobby table to me and said, "Hey, buddy. How much for first-class to Chicago?" He looked hurt when I told him that I wasn't a postal employee, and that rain, sleet, and snow were hell on crushed velvet.

"Before I forget, here's a present from Lorenz Novak," Cate said, handing me a cassette tape in a plastic box. On the label was a head-and-shoulders photo of Novak laughing. I covered the lower part of his face with my hands and looked at his eyes. They were hard, almost cruel.

"He says it's cued up to the instructions on how to relax."

"Yeah, he's a master at that," I said.

"After that comes the section on quitting smoking. Here's a tape player he gave me, too."

A corrugated steel window next to the mail slots rolled up high enough for a postal employee to stick his face through. He said, "Callahan? Anyone here named Harry Callahan?"

Harry Callahan? That's all I need to make my day.

"My name's Harry *Colderwood*. What can I do for you?" I bent my head sideways so I could see him better.

"No, this phone call's for someone named Callahan. What? Oh sorry," he said into his phone. To me, he said, "It *is* for a Harry Colderwood."

I reached for the phone, but he pulled it away. "Against regulations for me to even raise this window. We closed at five, but they put on extra shifts because of, you know, *tonight*. They could fire me for paging people like I was a bellboy."

My neck kinked from so much tilting. I sighed and said, "How much?"

He pretended puzzlement. I spelled it out. "How much did the man on the phone promise you I'd slip you under the table—I mean under the window?"

"A hundred."

"Ten dollars," I said.

"Fifty."

"Ten. Firm."

"You got it," he said.

"After I talk." It was his turn to sigh.

He slid me the receiver and shut the window on the phone cord. "Knock when you're finished," his muffled voice said.

I counted out ten ones and gave them to Cate. "You know what to do with these," I said. She nodded, no explanation necessary. God, we were such a team.

"Stanley," I said into the phone. "How the hell did you track me down?"

"By making AT&T rich. Tell me, yes or no. Are you doing anything at that post office to make us look bad?"

"I don't need this, Stanley. I got a TV crew coming and—"

His tirade drowned me out.

"Stanley, it's poor grammar to use run-on sentences."

I didn't tell him that the TV crew was from *Magazine Tonite*. They were in town to cover Quimp's announcement of his replacement and were willing to shoot an extra segment for me. Any TV coverage at this point in my career was a bonus.

I popped Novak's cassette in his recorder and pressed Play. Novak's voice oozed out of the speaker, coaxing the listener into relaxation. I laid the phone down next to it. Maybe someday Stanley Trimble would record a cassette tape of his threatening insults and sell it to people who want to have coronaries before age forty.

"Did Spillman like your Milking Routine?" I asked Cate.

"It went fine, but who knows what Spillman's looking for? One day away from naming his successor, and he still can't tell us apart when we're in makeup. Today he gave us each name tags with the wrong names on them. For forty-five minutes he called everyone by the wrong name, refusing to let us correct him. He thought I was Bill Rupeka."

The window rolled up again. "Done with the phone?" the postman said.

I turned off the recorder and picked up the receiver. Dial tone. "Yeah. Thanks."

"Hey. Where's my ten dollars?"

"Cate?" She handed him her ten-dollar purchase.

"Stamps? What the hell am I going to do with—" He slammed the window, cutting off his voice.

"So Spillman had the name tags all mixed up," I said. "That's interesting. You know, the same thing could have happened with—"

The post-office doors opened, and the television crew stormed the lobby. I introduced myself to *Magazine Tonite*'s Les Cook and asked if we could hold off until just before midnight. He refused. Within two minutes the room was hot with light, and I was speaking into a microphone with the *MT* logo on it.

" . . . so I thought your viewers might like to see what a magician does on April 15," I said.

Cook, in his early twenties, had a voice that sounded forty. His red hair, rich in lacquer, looked painted on his head.

In person, Cook's delivery seemed wooden. He smiled at everything and everybody but me. When he did deign to look at me, his eyes settled on my forehead. I knew that by the time his image reached viewers' living rooms, it would have the illusion of warmth. And that's what really counted.

"Viewers may remember when Harry Colderwood floated across the Grand Canyon on TV," Cook said.

I tried to explain he had me mixed up with another magician, but it would have been easier to stop a locomotive with my bare hands.

"Eight years ago Harry caused every piece of livestock in a small circus to vanish."

Not my greatest claim to fame, and it was more like ten years ago, when Les was probably in the sixth grade.

"Yes. Time flies. And flying time *is* my theme for tonight," I said. "Many people wait until the last minute to file their income tax. We magicians are no different . . . except when it comes to *mailing* our tax forms. Before I begin, let me tell you about a special treat in store for you tomorrow, in addition to the naming of the new Quimp the Clown."

This caught Cook by surprise. When he nodded, almost imperceptibly, to his cameraman, I knew I was free to go on.

I said, "Tomorrow evening, when Quimp crowns his successor, I will perform a classic illusion for the first time in five years. Working with me will be Cate Elliott Fleming, my former partner, who is now a full-time actress." No thanks to her agent, I thought.

Cook picked up the cue. "You two are back together again?"

"No. Just for tomorrow. Right, Cate?" The camera and lights swung toward her. She hunched her shoulders.

"What magic can we expect tomorrow?"

"I'll keep you in suspense," I said.

"Is it dangerous?"

"Yes, so risky that you must promise me something."

"Yes?"

"Should there be a tragic mishap, promise not to broadcast the results."

"Sorry. We won't cover your triumphs if we have to ignore your setbacks."

"You *would* call death a setback, wouldn't you, Les? Your coverage of Jolly Hands Justin was real Pulitzer Prize-caliber."

Jolly Hands, now in rehabilitative therapy, made his last performance on *Magazine Tonite*. His specialty was juggling chain saws, but he made more money peddling cocaine. Some racket boys, taking umbrage when he muscled in on their territory, secretly inserted weights in his chain saws, throwing them off balance. The results weren't pretty, but *Magazine Tonite* ran the segment anyway, airing lurid warnings all day. The show got record-high ratings, possibly due to the warnings.

Cook switched hands to better grip his mike. The cameraman stuck his head out from behind the camera to see if the announcer wanted to stop. Hand at his side, Cook made rapid circles with his forefinger: keep running.

Through clamped, picket-fence teeth, he said, "Don't fuck with us, Colderwood. Just do your simple-ass trick so we can get back to the party at our motel. I had hoped this spot would be easy to edit."

I offered him five dollars for a copy of the videotape with his profanity uncensored. He said he'd be glad to donate it . . . to my estate, along with tomorrow's recording of my demise.

"My demise? Is that a prophecy?"

"No. It's wishful thinking."

"Good, because I hardly believe in the future *itself*, let alone predicting it."

Last-minute tax filers still straggled in. Fascinated by the TV camera, they bottlenecked between the change machines and the mailing slots. They became my audience.

I cleared a space at a long table normally used for stamp licking, address writing, and zip-code checking. From my coat pocket I laid out tonight's tools of the trade: a ballpoint pen that looked like a magic wand, an envelope with a Day-Glo rainbow, and my 1040 forms.

I made semicircles in the air with my hands, as if conducting a miniature orchestra. In my head I played the "Funeral March of a Marionette." I hoped the studio would later dub in similar music on the tape.

The pen moved. All by itself.

The crowd hushed, and Cook motioned to the cameraman to tighten the shot. The pen floated six inches off the table and stopped.

It clicked, exposing the point, then continued its flight. Drifting lazily like a balloon, it hovered above my tax form.

Cook intruded upon the scene and waved a hand above the pen, searching for threads. None.

I shook my finger in mock admonition, then I sicked the pen on him. It scrawled blue lines on his hand until he backed away.

The pen executed a perfect one-point landing on the 1040's signature line. I coaxed it with my hands, but didn't touch it. In one continuous smooth motion, it signed my name to the form. The pen zipped into the air, did a triple-gainer, and landed in my coat pocket.

Next the tax form came to life. It folded itself into threes, slithered over to the envelope, and inserted itself. The envelope became airborne, and the cameraman pivoted hard, trying to keep it in his viewfinder. The audience applauded as the envelope soared to the row of mail slots and almost slipped itself into the one marked OUT OF TOWN. It zoomed back to me. Treading air at my side, the envelope's flap flipped open. I stuck out my tongue and it glided past, brushing my tongue, moistening its glue.

The envelope did a victory lap around the lobby, moved its flap up and down in a hurried goodbye, then sealed itself. Like an arrow finding its target, it shot into the mail slot.

The crowd cheered until someone said, "Holy shit. It's one minute till."

They charged the mail slots, having a brief shoving match, but they all managed to mail their envelopes on time. Thwacking sounds came from the other side of the wall where workers hand-stamped postmarks to ensure against late-filing penalties from Uncle Sam.

Cook moved into camera range and, hiding his inked hand in his pants pocket, did a speedy wrap-up. When the lights died, he handed his mike to his cameraman and stalked out, head turned away from me.

Cate came over, gave me a peck on the cheek, and said, "Bravo, Harry."

It was different this time. After a publicity stunt, I usually pulsed with excitement, hyperactive with the rush of victory.

Instead, my mind was preoccupied with clowns wearing the wrong name tags. And clues hidden in stacks of magic memorabilia.

And murder.

CHAPTER TWENTY-THREE

Alone. In my secret room in the Fitch.

After leaving the post office, my magic clothes felt oppressively heavy, and I was glad to shed them. I put everything on hangers, except my tux shirt. Still damp, it hung on the bathroom doorknob.

Sitting on a cushion made from my rolled-up sleeping bag, I opened the plastic box containing Novak's cassette. It included, "at no extra cost," a folded color poster of Novak—a wide-angle shot of him sitting at a typewriter in a living-room-size office. On his lapel was one of those smile buttons that indiscriminately wishes everyone a happy day. Only, this button was diamond-studded. The button's smile was effortless. Novak's wasn't.

Below the picture were quotes praising Novak's works, sources identified by only initials. It was comforting to know that B.K.K., M.B., and J.T. all adored Novak.

"Let's see what H.C. thinks," I said to the photo. I rewound the tape to the beginning and hit Play.

The intro was straight from *Mantovani's Greatest Hits*. As it faded, my phone rang, and I shut off the recorder. Picking up the phone, I heard a familiar grind and whirr, sounding like—

"Harry Colderwood, please."

—Cate's exercise bike, the kind her husband manufactured.

"This wouldn't be Phil Fleming, would it?" I asked.

The whirring stopped. "How the hell . . . ? You really *are* a magician." He was breathing hard.

I pictured him as having pumped up, bronze arms and a polished, hairless chest. His skin would be drawn tight like a hot dog's, a sheer wrapping for his traveling muscle museum. I wondered how he knew which room I was in. I had told no one but Cate.

"What can I do for you, Phil?"

"I want to get in touch with Cate. She's not answering her phone," he said, now breathing normally.

So you call me?

"The clowns must still be in session," I said.

"It's one in the morning."

"You obviously don't know Quimp. Stranger things have happened here lately." I didn't know if he was aware of Vaughn's death.

"How's that?" Suspicion tightened his voice.

"Nothing. It's been hectic for everyone, especially the clowns. I'll give Cate your message."

"*If* you run into her. Right?"

"Uh. Right."

The whirring resumed, and he talked between grunts. "Just tell her I want her to call. And that I—that I hope she wins."

"What's your number?"

"I'm at home. She knows her own number, believe me."

Then why hasn't she called you?

In the background, *Don Giovanni* suddenly competed with the bike's noise. He must have pressed the remote control of his sound system. So Fleming was the kind of guy who couldn't do just one thing at a time. His phone was probably cordless, with call-waiting, so he could put six people on hold at once.

With barely suppressed rage, he said, "Colderwood, is there something you want to tell me about—"

I stopped him before he went too far.

"Phil, when you run into a former employee, you don't ignore him, do you?"

"I don't understand."

"That's what Cate is to me: a former employee. No more. No less."

He was now pedaling like hell, and I waited a long minute for his reply. Barely audible, he coolly thanked me for my time and clicked off.

I kept the phone to my ear for a few moments. I laid it down, off the hook, not wanting him to call back.

A magician isn't proud of all his deceptions.

I didn't know how long I sat staring at my walls of taped notes. I dialed 0; and Jack, up late doing office work, answered. I asked if he had handled any outside calls to Cate's room in the last few hours. He said no, but that he did connect Phil Fleming's call to me. Jack asked me how Fleming had known which room to call.

Cate answered her phone on the first ring.

"Some questions, Cate. Please don't ask for any explanation right now."

"Go ahead."

"Has your husband contacted you since you arrived in Roselle?"

It caught her off guard.

"He called once, during the convention, and that's when I told him about the clown auditions."

"You never called him back?"

"What's this have to do with—oh, skip it. Harry, this is Phil's busy season. He's finalizing promotions for next year's winter line, and I don't want to interrupt him."

"Does he know I'm here?"

"No. You showed up *after* I talked with him. Harry, is Phil bothering you?"

No, but my conscience sure as hell is.

I told her I'd explain later. I hoped she wouldn't hold me to that promise.

* * *

Rupeka's number was busy. I hit the receiver button, but didn't hang up.

I unrolled my sleeping bag, stretched out on top of it, and again started the recorder. A pudding-voiced announcer introduced me to Lorenz Novak's *Smoke-Stop* tape. His voice blended with the dial tone of the off-the-hook phone, lulling me.

I lit a cigarette.

The first segment on the tape was the audio portion of Novak's appearance on *The David Letterman Show*. Letterman played Novak for laughs, but most of the host's taunts and quips were crudely edited out. The audience's laughter remained uncut (for medical purposes, of course). The unintentional result was a heightened listener curiosity about the censored lines.

In concluding the interview, Novak demonstrated his mind's supposed control over his body—he "stopped" his heart. Letterman and an audience volunteer couldn't find Novak's pulse until, seemingly at will, he restarted his heart.

His audacity galled me. I used to perform this same stunt at college parties, and it had nothing to do with voodoo, mind power, or anything else exotic. Most libraries had books explaining this not-so-secret secret.

More simpering music followed the interview before Novak's voice reappeared, lower and more controlled than in the Letterman segment. He explained that the following relaxation exercises should be done in a comfortable setting and not, for safety reasons, in a car.

He asked me to close my eyes. With the reverence of an art curator guiding me through a gallery of treasures, he identified various parts of my body, asking me to envision them undergoing odd changes. For example, I imagined my stomach as a gradually deflating tire and my arms as sledgehammers, too heavy to lift. As he evoked images of heaviness for the rest of my anatomy, I felt silly.

But it worked. The mainspring in my gut gradually loosened, and I felt myself stepping outside of the jumbled mess of the past days.

At Novak's suggestion, I scanned distant memories, choosing a time of innocence and freedom. I was floating— sleeping without actually being asleep.

With effort, I shut off the recorder, my arm weighing a ton. I wanted quiet while savoring the scene I was about to relive.

I was nine years old again, and for the first time, performing for someone other than my family. My audience-of-one was Mr. Kaufman, owner of the confectionery store around the corner from our house. I made sponge rabbits appear and disappear from his hand. At the trick's climax, Mr. Kaufman opened his hand, and it overflowed with baby sponge rabbits. I watched not his hand, but the real magic— the usually dour storekeeper was grinning like a kid.

Mr. Kaufman shook my hand as if I had just passed a milestone in my life as important as graduating from college. After that I became family to Mr. Kaufman. Years later, when I was appearing on TV, he'd brag to his customers about how he had given me my start. Until his death a few years ago, he regularly mailed me updates on the old neighborhood.

I was back in time again. This was no vague, fleeting memory. I felt as if I were *there*.

I could see Kaufman's cracked candy case, more tape than glass. I smelled its heavy-sweet odor. I shifted my feet on the loose floorboards that always creaked louder when I was trying to sneak something without paying. All the old guys were there, the ones who hung out, talking baseball, drinking coffee, and helping Mr. Kaufman with odd jobs.

I relived the dreams that were inside that nine-year-old boy—dreams of performing magic before millions on the television.

I willed my hand to restart the tape, but it lay useless at my side. I wanted to stay there inside Kaufman's forever, but my subconscious mind had other plans. The store did a slow dissolve.

My eyes fluttered open and stared at my wallpaper of notes. Like windows slamming, my eyelids went shut again. The facts of the Vaughn case slowly shuffled themselves in my head. Bits and pieces bobbed to the surface, only to sink again into my mind's caldron. Each thought melted and was replaced by another before I could consider it. It would have been easier to chase a solitary snowflake during a storm.

The mental flashes came and went:

Ratcliff, the actor, daubing clown makeup on Vaughn.

The computer terminal in Tarrant's office.

Rupeka lurking in the hallway outside of Cate's room.

Mrs. Ames saying she once lived in Montana and recently had moved again unexpectedly.

The flashes then came in a flood:

Michelle Blue's bluebird tattoo.

The burglar telling me that Tarrant wheeled something out of his office.

A severely burned Novak on his deathbed, mapping his future on the talk-show circuit.

The nude of Michelle on the cell wall.

The hitchhiker murderer in the next county.

The empty capsule package in Ames's room.

More, faster:

The attack on Hodge.

Rupeka and his gun.

Ames's skin ointment.

The group pictures in the basement.

A bearded man in one of those fuzzy, faded pictures becoming more distinct until he looked like a young Lorenz Novak. The caption below the photograph: Rock Tabernacle Church.

The call from Cate's husband.

The clowns wearing the wrong name tags.

The mental pictures now blurred, with a final image lingering: Vaughn's body curled up in the safe. He opened his eyes, winked, and silenced me with a finger to its lips.

As that picture drifted away, I became aware of a sensation in my fingers. I rolled my head to the right and saw that my cigarette, now a long ash, was burning my fingers. It barely tingled. I dropped it on the floor, feeling weightless. Peaceful.

I tried to remember why I was lying atop my sleeping bag in this strange hotel room.

Oh yes. The tape.

I turned the recorder back on and spent the next fifteen minutes listening to Novak's stop-smoking suggestions. His words barely registered.

At the end of the tape, I stood up and stretched, fatigue gone. I stepped on my dropped cigarette to make sure it was out. I put a fresh one in my mouth and steadied my lighter near it, watching the edge of the white paper turn brown. I put my lighter away and replaced the cigarette in the pack. My fingers moved automatically, as when executing a sleight I've known for years.

"I'll be damned."

I now realized who murdered Vaughn. And why. I felt no victory, just relief.

Novak's tape had worked. *Too* well.

It would land his ass in jail, where he'd have plenty of time to write books and make inspirational tapes. He'd just have to cut back considerably on the personal appearances.

I made more phone calls, one to a tobacco shop in Philadelphia, the other an urgent message to the Frontier Hotel in Las Vegas. Then I called Sam Wirfel.

"Listen carefully, Deputy. You and the sheriff will be present tomorrow for the crowning of the new Quimp. Don't interrupt me. The sheriff *will* be there, because you are going to tell him exactly what I'm about to tell you. Just be sure he thinks you don't believe me."

* * *

I called the Rock Tabernacle, an independent church in Roselle.

The groggy-voiced man that answered the parsonage phone was miffed by the late hour, and I begged him not to hang up. As I asked my questions, he seemed to forget the time.

"We're a new church. Been here for six years," he said.

"What about the Rock Tabernacle that was in Roselle decades ago?"

"It closed its doors about fifteen years ago. When we started our present church, we used their former building. The name Rock Tabernacle was above the entrance in stone, so we adopted the name of the original church. Now I wish we would change our name and completely rid any confusion between us and that first tabernacle," he said acidly.

I wanted to find out what was distasteful about that first church. "Are there any records from the original Rock?"

"No, they've long since been destroyed, but our church treasurer, a member of the local historical society, has taken an interest in the former church."

I jotted down the treasurer's phone number on the nearest piece of paper—Novak's picture.

I explained my plan to Spillman in his room. In pajamas, he sat on the edge of his chair. In spite of his yawning, he was performing the coin trick flawlessly—no dropping or flashing.

"There's no other way to do this?" he asked.

"No, we need all those people in one place."

"Sounds dangerous."

"It'll be finished shortly after you announce your successor, so it will all be on tape. By the way, have you decided on the new Quimp yet?"

He looked pained. "Soon, soon."

He repeated the coin sleight, this time doing it with his eyes closed.

"Beautiful, Marcus," I said. "Did you get more coaching?"

He nodded.

"From Novak again?" I asked.

"Yes."

"Is that an astringent you're using to improve your grip?"

He shook his head. "Why?"

"I just thought I smelled something."

"I don't smell a thing," he said.

He agreed to have each clown bring his hand props for the Milking Routine tomorrow, and I left him to play with his coin. I knew he'd be up all night endlessly repeating the coin trick while agonizing over his choice of successor. I had a hunch that, come five in the morning, he'd say "To hell with it," and flip his damn coin a few times to get the decision over with.

I'd be up all night, too, but not flipping a coin. Just turning over an old Rock to see what was underneath.

Outside Spillman's room, I passed Novak, and he asked me where I was going so late.

"Church," I said.

Looking at me with tired disgust, he shuffled back to his room before I could tell him how well his tape worked. Or which church I was going to.

Because the shadows concealed him, I heard him before I saw him. He had been standing around the corner from the entrance to the Fitch.

"When do I start?" he said as the front door glided closed behind me.

"That was a quick trip. What the hell did you do? Rent a plane from Philadelphia?"

"Never made it back there. I stuck around to watch you work. And to figure our your game. When I checked in by phone with my Philadelphia contact, he said you tried to contact me. Well, aren't you going to welcome me aboard?"

"Let's talk money first."

He quoted his fee, saying, "That's low, because I owe you for springing me. What do you need a professional burglar for?"

"I doubt there are many locks you can get past faster than me, but I need someone who knows what to do *after* the locks are picked—someone who's good at finding things."

I told him the rest. He smiled and said it sounded like fun.

CHAPTER TWENTY-FOUR

Cate and I sat in the former bar of the Fitch Hotel. For the third time this morning I slipped a cigarette into my lips and fired up my lighter—then shut the lid and put the cigarette away. Cate looked at me in wonder, but made no mention of my sudden conversion.

We both dressed for the occasion: she as Quimp and me as the struggling magician. My rumpled tuxedo was long overdue for the cleaners.

I looked at the goggles, leather gloves, and the plate of glass on the table. The glass was two feet square and a quarter-inch thick. The gloves and goggles would protect me if the glass broke during today's performance.

"I'd feel safer if it were live TV, not just tape," Cate said.

"Live TV's long dead. It's the *tape* I'm interested in today. A taped confession would be strong in court."

"Even so, you still can't entirely prove your case."

"Not yet. I have crucial evidence that's, shall we say, in transit."

"I've done some deducing myself, Harry. I know who the next Quimp will be."

The look she gave me was so superior, I decided not to ask for her prediction.

I slid the bottle to the center of the table and said, "If we were doing straight magic, I'd suggest something stronger. But under these circumstances we need all our wits."

Cate opened the bottle of diet cola and poured it into plastic cocktail glasses. We toasted each other.

Then she removed the Smith & Wesson .44 Special from her prop bag and dry-fired it at her reflection in the bar mirror. I patted my coat pocket to make sure the ammo was there.

On my way out the barroom door, Jack stopped me and said, "I showed that photo you took of Sheriff Tarrant to the night clerk at Torme's. He recognized him as a frequent customer at his motel. Michelle Blue fits the description of the girl that always accompanied him," he said.

"How far away is Torme's?"

"A good forty miles. Far enough that the clerk has never heard of either Perry Vaughn or the sheriff. That information cost me fifty bucks."

I nodded.

He said, "I feel like slipping *you* fifty so you'll explain what it all means."

"You'll find out shortly."

"Here's more interesting news. On the way back I stopped at Michelle Blue's. There's a For Rent sign on her half of the duplex. I knocked and looked in the window. She's moved out."

I told Jack about her one-way ticket to Florida.

We looked across the lobby at the nervously chattering clowns, all wearing name tags. I again smelled the same petroleum odor as I had in Spillman's room. I spotted the source: Jack had placed two kerosene space heaters in the middle of the lobby. I figured he must be preparing to shut off the heat in the hotel.

I decided to put Rupeka at an immediate psychological disadvantage. I didn't need more complication. One unruly cop would be enough. I signaled to him, and he followed me into the men's room off the hotel lobby.

Making sure we were alone, I said, "How much is Cate's husband paying you?"

Rupeka's painted face retained its clown smile, but his real lips tightened in shock. "You're nuts," he said.

I positioned myself so that, if necessary, I could slam the waste can in his face and retreat out the door.

"No more games. I don't know why they kicked you off the force in Weirton, but—"

"I resigned."

"The details don't matter. What matters is that Phil Fleming hired you to snoop on Cate. What's he afraid of? That when she makes the big time, she'll leave him in her dust?"

My face, now inches from his, burned. I told Rupeka that I suspected Cate's husband was meddling in her career, paying off her agent to screen out jobs that looked too promising or could send her too far away from his invisible tentacles . . . from the control he thrived on.

Rupeka said, "Harry, I know how you feel about Cate, and I respect that."

My angry rush of words lost steam, and I faltered. "How I . . . feel about her has nothing to do with this. I'm concerned about her *talent*. Show business is an impossible life. The breaks are few, and most come only once. I hate to see that bastard deny Cate her due."

Rupeka's necktie sprang up in my face, and I reflexively snatched it, choking him.

"Accident," he said, pulling it out of my hands and resetting it.

"You got a lot of gags on you?" I asked.

"No, just enough for one routine. In case I win."

I wanted a cigarette, not for the nicotine, but because lighting it would give me a chance to study Rupeka's reactions. Instead, he lit up one and studied me. So much for his bid to quit smoking.

Because of his red clown lips, the smoke he exhaled looked whiter than normal. After a few moments, he said, "I apologize. To both you and Cate. I've never done anything like this before. Christ, I thought there was too much dirt in a cop's job. Just try detective work."

"You're serious about this competition? It's not a cover?"

He nodded. "It's the only reason I stayed behind after the Magicade. When Cate told her husband that one of the clown finalists was a cop, he couldn't resist. I thought Fleming was joking when he called me on the phone. Only when his courier arrived with the packet of money did I believe him. At first I thought Fleming was an eccentric who wanted to keep a detailed log of his wife's bed games, but now I agree with you that Fleming is a control freak."

I searched his candy-colored face for some remnant of the macho cop I knew, the one with the rock-hard arms and knife-scarred body. "You're shaking," I said.

He checked his rising necktie again, then knelt to tie the lace on his clown shoe. "Stage fright."

"Yeah. Me too," I said.

"I returned Fleming's money this morning by fourth-class parcel post. I couldn't afford a courier."

He pulled his gun from his ankle holster, and I reached for the trash can. Too late. He pulled the trigger.

It made an *owwoooga* sound. Quimp used the same kind of gun in his Keystone Klown Kop routine. He laughed at his gag. I didn't.

"What now?" I asked.

"I'm going to stay out of the way and watch a magician crack a murder."

"You've been eavesdropping?"

"From the very beginning. We're living in a world of electronic wonders, aren't we?"

"And what if this magician screws up?"

"Then this Keystone Klown will come to his rescue." He clapped his hands. Like a window blind, his other pant leg rolled up. His real pistol was holstered on that ankle.

I examined his fake clown gun. "German?"

"Swiss. Cost almost as much as my real gun and may even be better made."

"I hope not."

Before we left the restroom, he said, "For what it's

worth, I didn't tell Fleming anything personal about you and Cate. I just said you two were temporarily resurrecting your magic act."

My face turned clown-red without the aid of makeup.

Out in the lobby, Les Cook and his TV crew had arrived and were checking equipment, trying to pick the best place to shoot without getting any of the lobby's remaining crates in the picture. Rupeka joined the other clowns who were sitting on chairs, talking to Jack. In front of the registration desk, Sheriff Tarrant and Deputy Wirfel stood vigil.

Each clown had brought props, all agreeing the new Quimp should perform his own rendition of his favorite Quimp routine. I already knew that Rupeka had chosen the Klown Kop routine. Cate had brought everything for the Milking Routine, including the milk can and the fake ice pick. Novak had a seltzer bottle between his legs, prepared for a sketch entitled "Thirsty!" Hodge had no props, unless he was concealing something in his arm sling.

Cate pulled me aside. "Rupeka *quit* the police force."

"I know. He told me."

"I just got off the phone with a reporter from a newspaper in Weirton. He said you called earlier, leaving a message inquiring about Rupeka. He claims Rupeka lied to us, that he only briefly did school assemblies before going back to active service on the force. He also said that six months ago Rupeka went home sick in the middle of his night shift and found a man in bed with his wife."

"What happened?"

"The guy, thinking Rupeka was a prowler, pretended he was armed. His bluff worked—Rupeka shot him through the eye. Internal Affairs cleared Rupeka of any wrongdoing, but he soon developed emotional troubles on the job, including a few locker-room fights. They pulled him off street duty and gave him desk work, but Rupeka quit soon after that. The reporter thinks that Rupeka probably has not recovered yet."

Grinning his moronic clown grin, Rupeka came over and said, "Cook's ready. He wants to roll 'em."

I was curious if Rupeka's own private internal affairs had cleared him. I also wondered what he really thought about Cate and me, since his own wife's affair had ended so violently. I now wished I had flattened his forehead with the garbage can and taken his gun—the real one—when I had the chance.

Cate gave her own gun a last-minute check.

As Cook did a sound check, my tongue traced the dried edges of my lips, and my stomach knotted. All good signs. Stage fright and I are old friends. Its absence before a performance truly alarms me.

I asked the cameraman how long his recorder would run without reloading, and I decided it was adequate. He said since he despised Cook he would point the camera wherever I wanted. I think the twenty-dollar bill I slipped in his shirt pocket helped persuade him, too. My wink would be his cue to swing his camera.

The cameraman clapped his hands, and the lobby quieted. I briefed Cook on Cate's and my trick, telling him nothing, however, of our unscheduled performance.

"Good evening," Cook said into the camera, with the hush of a golf announcer. "In addition to the crowning of a new Quimp the Clown, we have another treat. Entertainment teams have come and gone: Martin and Lewis, Olson and Johnson, and Simon and Schuster. For today only, the magic team of Harry Colderwood and Cate Elliott Fleming is back again. The *Magazine Tonite* camera will catch it all for you."

And how.

Cook had failed to note that today would also mark the breakup of yet one more show-business team: Marcus Spillman and Quimp the Clown. In costume for the last time, Spillman joined Cook before the camera.

"Tell us, Marcus, why are you giving up the greasepaint?"

Spillman eyed him with forced patience. "I will devote an entire chapter to that subject in my new book."

"Cagey, aren't you? Couldn't resist that advance plug. Folks, Mr. Spillman has already penned one book, *Clowning and Living*. What's the name of this new one?"

"*Life and the Vegas Close-up Magician*. I haven't started writing it, though. I have to succeed in Vegas as a close-up magician, first."

"I see. Before bestowing the name of Quimp on another clown this evening, what will be your last act?"

"This."

Spillman's eyes glossed, and the lobby grew still. He said, "I think . . . I want . . . some Kool Aid."

We moved back to give him room.

"I think . . . *grape* Kool Aid would be nice."

Marcus Spillman turned his back on us. When his face was completely hidden, he paused. As he faced us again, his jerking movement reminded me of a movie with missing frames. He was no longer Marcus Spillman. He was now Quimp the Clown, for the last time.

All of us had seen the routine before. With invisible utensils and ingredients, he made himself an imaginary pitcher of Kool-Aid and "poured" himself a glass. Next came the part I always studied. Even if I were to rewatch it a hundred times, the effect would still be electric.

All he did was pantomime drinking his glass of soft drink. It was no longer imaginary, but not quite real, either—somewhere in between. In my mind's eye, I vividly saw it. We all did.

Some of the drink even dribbled down his chin. He wiped it off, making a "purple" stain on his face and hand. He licked his lips and then accidentally dropped the glass. He "cut" himself picking up the broken pieces.

Without one tangible prop, he seduced us into seeing and hearing. I nearly tasted the tart grape flavor myself. With a lay audience, he usually got belly laughs with this routine. From us, it earned reverent silence.

This was the man who was giving up clowning to do

magic. Didn't he realize this and all his other routines *were* magic?

To end the sketch, he usually took a low bow, still sucking his thumb. However, this time he removed his finger from his mouth, finding a gold coin perched atop it.

The coin dissolved into air, then reappeared between his first two fingers. He tossed it to the floor with disdain. Another appeared, and he threw it down. He repeated it again and again, accumulating a trove of gold coins at his feet. He took a deep bow.

My applause outlasted everyone's, and I was ashamed of ever doubting his ability. Spillman will make it to Vegas, I thought.

His voice hoarse, as if he had been coughing hard, Cook resumed announcing. Without knowing exactly what he had witnessed, he had been swept up in the audience's spirit. He walked across the layers of coins to join Spillman.

"The time has come. Who will be your successor?" Cook said.

Spillman's voice boomed. "The new Quimp will be Gregory Hodge, the collector of magic curios."

Acknowledging the smattered applause, Hodge stepped forward and slipped on the coins. One of his clown shoes fell off, and he landed on his buttocks with none of the grace of a good pratfall.

I looked at Cate questioningly, and she beamed. Her prediction had come true.

It made sense. The role of Quimp was now permanently retired, like Stan Musial's number. At the same time, Hodge had just added the biggest prize to his collection— total ownership of the title of Quimp. Now only Hodge was authorized to portray him.

Spillman could rest easy knowing that no one would ever do a second-rate job performing the character he had created. Hodge probably never wanted to play the role of Quimp; he just wanted to *collect* it. Also, Spillman got national publicity for the launch of his close-up magic career.

Staring at Cook's microphone, Hodge humbly accepted the honor, saying that at the moment he preferred not to perform anything as the new Quimp.

Recovered from his rare moment of on-camera emotion, Cook again found his bass voice and asked for another round of applause for Hodge. Then he said, "If in the next three minutes someone were to fire a gun at your face, what would you do? Duck? Run? Pull out a gun of your own? What kind of man stands his ground and smiles? A madman? Perhaps. Or a *magician.* Harry Colderwood and Cate Fleming will now perform the Man with the Bulletproof Smile."

While Cook talked on, spinning his long, fat sentences, Cate displayed the Smith & Wesson pistol and a tray containing bullets, a knife, goggles, my leather gloves, and the pane of glass.

Sheriff Tarrant performed the duty he thought we'd invited him for: he examined the gun and bullets and declared them genuine. Camera shy, he spoke in a meek mumble.

Cate got Marcus Spillman to choose a bullet and mark it with the knife. Cate took the bullet from him and, in passing, muttered, "Morbid son of a bitch." I saw that Spillman had scratched an ace of spades—a death symbol—on the bullet's surface.

Cate set down the tray and handed the bullet to the sheriff who loaded it in the gun. The TV lights bleached Tarrant's face. Hands trembling, he dropped the bullet and stooped to retrieve it.

Someone moved in the shadows behind Tarrant—amid the stacks of crates. It was a man whose natural habitat was shadows: the burglar. I bet even his mug shots were underexposed, with only his eyes and pale cheeks visible.

He waved a brown padded envelope at me and laid it on a sheet-covered lobby chair. As I nodded, he waved farewell, walking away into (what else?) the shadows.

Still kneeling, Tarrant found the marked bullet. After he

loaded the gun, his confidence picked up. "Hold it. I want to check the firearm again," he said to Cook.

He assumed a formal marksman's stance: body turned to the side, free hand on waist, pistol pointed to the ceiling. He lowered it and took aim . . . *at me*. The lights' glare made him appear cold, impersonal.

I went rigid.

Click.

I don't know if I flinched on the outside when the hammer hit the empty chamber, but *everything* flinched on the inside.

Tarrant let go a singsong chuckle and said, "I knew the live round wasn't in the chamber." He handed the firearm to Cate, then stepped back beside Wirfel and folded his arms.

After donning the leather gloves and protective goggles, I lifted the pane of glass over my head and rotated for all to see. I lowered it to the front of my face, with my nose nearly touching it. I had to control my breathing so the glass wouldn't fog.

"Ladies and gentlemen, the Bullet-Catching Feat is a classic . . . and a killer," Cook said. "Colderwood informed me that many conjurors have been maimed, and some have died, attempting it."

My mind drifted away from Cook's speech. I rubbed the mist off the glass with my bow tie. It was like watching the whole thing through a television screen.

Cook went on. "Magic historians say Houdini wanted to do bullet-catching—"

Using a two-handed combat grip, Cate aimed at my face.

My eyes shifted focus to my reflection in the glass. I positioned my teeth in the proper open-mouthed smile.

"—but his friends talked him out of it, thinking it was a foolhardy misuse of his talents."

All eyes on me, I winked at the cameraman, and he gave a quick wave. As requested, he gradually changed his angle away from Cate and me until he now focused on Sheriff Tarrant. The publicity potential of our stunt was now destroyed.

I watched Tarrant take slow quarter-steps, staying on his

toes. He glided behind Cate, who was taking pains to aim the pistol. At first I thought the sheriff's hand was in his pocket, but I realized it was on his gun.

Cate widened her stance, and we exchanged nods. Tarrant ducked behind one of the crates and used it to steady his aim at my chest.

I closed my eyes tight, seeing only a crimson tint from the TV lights.

"The bullet has been marked. Cate Fleming has zeroed in on her quarry . . ."

Why doesn't Cook clam up? Does he think his viewers are blind?

Gunfire. The glass in my hand jolted but didn't shatter. My head snapped back, and my neck burned. Whiplash. I knew this was my last bullet-catch.

I opened my eyes but couldn't see through the glass. In the center was a bullet hole with cracks jutting from it. I lowered the pane, and Cook rushed up to me. Jack was at his side, holding the tray.

Cook asked me how I felt, but I couldn't talk with a bullet between my teeth. I spit it out onto the tray.

"Get a close-up of this, Ray. By God, this *is* the original slug. It has the spade insignia that Marcus Spillman scratched on it. Ray? Where the hell's Ray?"

Ray was busy shooting what I had asked him to. He finally heeded his boss and swung his camera our way. After Ray moved, I could see Tarrant again. Cook spouted off about the "miracle" that had just taken place.

I noted the blank shock on Tarrant's face. Wirfel stood behind him, his lips forming words I couldn't hear. I knew that when I later examined Cate's gun, there would be an extra spent shell inside it—the one Tarrant had secretly inserted, hoping it would explain why everyone heard *two* shots, instead of one. He wanted it to seem that Cate had accidentally fired an extra shot, killing me. Wirfel had pulled his own gun in time to prevent Tarrant from firing that second shot.

The glass plate slipped from my hands, smashing. I made it to Cate in two steps, and we clumsily embraced. I still wore the leather gloves and goggles, and she hadn't relinquished her grip on the gun. As Jack passed, I took off my protective gear and put them on the tray. Cate laid the pistol beside them.

We kissed. Long and passionately. The camera swung our way and caught it all. I hoped Phil Fleming wouldn't.

When we broke our embrace, I saw that Wirfel held two guns. One was the deputy's service revolver. The other was Tarrant's.

"Ladies and gentlemen, what you just witnessed—holy shit! What's going on?" Cook said when he saw Wirfel's guns.

I clucked my tongue. "Now you're going to have to edit again, Les."

"Turn the camera off, Ray."

"Keep taping, Ray," I said.

Ray obeyed me. The clowns edged away at the sight of the guns.

"Would someone explain what the hell's going on?" Cook said.

"Okay, Les. If you really insist."

If there had been burning logs in the lobby fireplace, I would have poked them and told everyone to gather near to listen. Instead, I poked Cook in the ribs, took his microphone, and told everyone to stay put.

I took a deep breath. A hell of a deep breath.

"It all started with a dead clown, and it almost ended with a dead magician . . ."

it up, and Crowell recently repaid that favor by falsely
... then Months appeared in the safe. Crowell
... to that ... because there's ... with
...

CHAPTER TWENTY-FIVE

The only sound was the tape machine's steady hum.

I talked into the mike. "Testing. One, two, three. Much tape left, Ray?" He gave a thumbs-up.

Cook said, "Give me that. Who the hell do you think—"

"Shut up, Cook," Wirfel said.

Cook relented, not wanting to quibble with a man holding two guns. He busied himself, straightening his tie, then checking his wrist watch.

I said, "Four days ago a man wearing a clown suit was found dead in the hotel safe. We all thought he was Perry Vaughn, but we were wrong. You see, there were *two* murders—not just one. Vaughn was murdered later that evening."

"Mr. Colderwood, speak directly into the mike. My sound meter's barely moving."

"Certainly, Ray." I cleared my throat and spoke louder. "Perry Vaughn had dedicated his short life to spreading misery. No one misses him. In fact, this town unofficially declared a holiday after his death. But there's one man in Roselle who never gets a holiday: Sheriff Virgil Tarrant. Daily he must set aside personal feelings to do his job. However, in this case Tarrant let his personal feelings run wild. He murdered Vaughn."

"But the coroner said it was Vaughn in that safe and that he died accidentally," Jack said.

"Coroner Ted Crowell lied. A couple of years ago Crowell, driving drunk, hit and killed a little girl. Tarrant covered it up, and Crowell recently repaid that favor by falsely certifying that Vaughn smothered in the safe. Crowell, along with the undertaker, helped Sheriff Tarrant switch the body of the dead clown for Vaughn's at the funeral parlor.''

''Why would Tarrant kill Vaughn?'' Jack asked.

''Fear, mostly.'' I said ''Vaughn's calling in life was to be a bully, and he loved it. He even found a way to make it pay. Local businesses regularly gave him money *not* to harass them—all with Tarrant's secret blessing. For a piece of the action, he allowed Vaughn's game to flourish. He arrested Vaughn frequently, but only for show. However, their little racket started to fall apart when Tarrant became romantically involved with Vaughn's girl friend, Michelle Blue—a woman who, by her own admission, has a weakness for highly protective men. One of their secret meeting places was a motel called Torme's. When Vaughn found out about their affair he started physically abusing Michelle and publicly bad-mouthing Tarrant. Vaughn became a powder keg, ready to blow. Tarrant had lost control of him.''

Tarrant tried to stand erect, but his carriage now sagged, as though my words had pierced him. Wirfel warily drifted back a few steps beyond the sheriff's reach.

''When I visited Michelle Blue's house, I saw Vaughn's well-concealed sensitive side—his artwork. One of his works, a nude of Michelle, is still on a cell wall in the Roselle jail, even though Tarrant tried to scrub it off. Really burned you up to think of those two together, didn't it, Tarrant?''

Unarmed, Tarrant strained to maintain toughness. He said, ''What's the big deal about that picture?''

''In Vaughn's drawing, there's a tattoo of a bluebird on Michelle's buttock. She actually has such a tattoo, but it's only a few days old. She told me that Vaughn knew nothing about it until she surprised him with it. Vaughn must have occupied that cell some time *after* she got that tattoo.

Yet Tarrant said he hadn't seen Vaughn for several weeks. Why would he lie?''

"Cut. Hold it." It was Cook again. "Was Tarrant playing everything by ear or did he have this alleged crime all planned ahead of time?''

Alleged. Cook must have spent a day or two working a police beat.

"A little of both," I said. "Tarrant had been waiting for exactly the right crime to provide a smokescreen to conceal his murder of Vaughn. The unknown clown in the safe was perfect, and he dove at the opportunity. He and the coroner must have done some fast thinking while they were alone in the hotel office. After leaving the crime scene, Tarrant probably phoned Michelle's and learned that Vaughn was there alone. Then Tarrant picked him up and took him to his office. Nothing unusual—Tarrant often pretended to harass Vaughn as a cover to get his cut of the protection money.

"That night he tricked Vaughn, locking him in a cell. While Vaughn drew his little mural of Michelle, Tarrant called the funeral home and told Crowell to go ahead with their plan. Then he went back into the cell and snuffed Vaughn, probably with his bare hands to avoid the noise and mess of a gunshot. There was most likely a struggle, and that's how Tarrant got that cut above his eye. He stowed the body in the interviewing room after a store owner called to report he was holding a would-be burglar at gunpoint.

"After Tarrant returned with the burglar and locked him up, Garth Eyles, the undertaker, arrived to ship Vaughn's body to his mortuary." I recalled that the burglar had said he'd heard a door open, followed by something being wheeled across the floor. "Tarrant confiscated the burglar's set of tools and claimed that he had found them on Vaughn's body, figuring that would support his theory that Vaughn had broken into the Fitch."

Tarrant hungrily eyed Wirfel's two guns. Time for the coup de grâce. "By the way, Sheriff, Michelle's gone. Left town. She never even phoned you, did she? I bet her insurance money came today."

The sheriff edged forward menacingly until Wirfel gave his guns a warning shake.

"Yesterday the clowns got their name tags mixed up. Tarrant mixed up some tags too—only, in this case it was *body* tags. Tarrant did all his dirty work while Deputy Wirfel kept watch here at the hotel. The deputy was in the dark about the sheriff's games."

One of the clowns spoke. I recognized Rupeka's voice. "Tarrant killed them both—Vaughn *and* this guy in the safe?"

"No. The sheriff murdered only Vaughn. He had no idea of who killed the clown in the safe. The coroner and the undertaker removed the costume from the original corpse in the safe and dressed Vaughn's body in it so that bogus crime report photos could be taken. Tarrant then dumped the other body—the one found here at the hotel— at a site in the next county where victims of the Hitchhiker Murderer had been found nude. Sheriff, I'm sure you've been half crazy wondering who murdered the clown in the safe. All you could do was sweat it out until the clown competition ended and everybody went quietly home, including the unknown killer.

"The last thing you wanted was to solve the murder of the clown, so you decided to let matters ride, hoping that the other murderer understood—you weren't going to hassle him. It must have been terrifying to have your fate in tandem with his. You both would have been in the clear if I hadn't started asking questions . . . and if *someone else* hadn't been close to stumbling onto a clue."

"Who?" Tarrant said, looking melted.

"Gregory Hodge. Cataloguing the basement collection cost him a punch in the eye and a kick in the head. I barely escaped being blown up when I started probing down there, too."

"So who was this other corpse?" Rupeka asked.

"The dead man in the clown suit was Lloyd Ames, a

pharmaceutical salesman. Several nights ago we discovered that Ames had been secretly living in the hotel. It was *his* body that Tarrant dumped in the next county. I've asked police there to verify that corpse as Ames. Their ID isn't positive yet, but the chances look good. They're also running extra tests for traces of theatrical makeup on the corpse's skin.

"Also, Ames did not smother to death in that safe. Someone *stabbed* him before cramming him inside. All the victims of the mass murderer in the next county had also been stabbed—that's why Tarrant dumped the body there. Just one more victim on their list. Tell me, Marcus, what routine were the clowns working on the day the body was discovered?"

"The Milking Routine."

"Do you use sharp objects in that routine?"

"Not really. No, wait. *The ice pick.*"

"Yes. A stab from an ice pick would bleed only minimally. That's why none of us saw the wound on Ames's body. To cover up the cause of death, Tarrant thoroughly cleaned any trace of blood from the safe before returning it."

Spillman said, "But our ice picks are harmless. They only *appear* to stab a hole in the elbow for milk to stream out."

"Then I'm sure none of the clowns will object to an ice pick inspection."

They all nodded.

"Me too?" Spillman asked.

"Yes, you too. Les Cook's belly will be our proving ground."

"Now, hold on," Cook said.

"What's wrong, Les? Squeamish? Okay. *I'll* be the guinea pig. Follow me," I said to the cameraman.

I stopped in front of Spillman. "By the way, fine coin routine, Marcus. How about poking your ice pick right about here?" I pointed to a spot above my navel. Spillman shrugged and shoved his pick. Cook gasped. The shaft penetrated my midsection—at least it appeared to.

"Don't worry. All illusion," I said. "A standard magician's prop. Costs three dollars." I withdrew Spillman's pick, walked over to Cook, and "stabbed" his arm. "See?" He suppressed nervous laughter.

"Next."

I got similar results with Rupeka's pick and Hodge's.

Even Cate submitted to the test, but I thought she took far too much delight in running me through.

"Finally, let's give your ice pick a clean bill of health," I said to Lorenz Novak. "Not worried, are you?"

"Not at all," he said. "You've been so smug, it'll be a pleasure."

He took his ice pick out of his prop bag. As he ran his fingers along the shaft, his gloating turned to panic. With supreme effort he regained control of himself, saying, "If this pick's real, it won't mean a thing. *Anyone* could have planted it on me, including this phantom murderer you're ranting about. If I hurt you, it's not my fault. I'll have witnesses. Millions of them."

"Quit stalling. Take the plunge."

He lunged with his whole body, and the pick pierced my tux shirt. He thrust several times, but the pick would go no farther than an eighth of an inch into my shirt. Face crimson, Novak made one more furious attempt to gut me. Frustrated, he threw down the pick, sticking it in the floor. No fake.

I unbuttoned my shirt and reached inside.

"A new device that someday will be standard police issue for exposing clown murderers—the ice-pick-proof vest." From under my shirt I took out a book. *"Laughter, the Healthy O.D.* by Lorenz Novak. Informative book, but very hard to get through. As the author just demonstrated."

"You bastard. That's not the pick I put in my bag today. You *planted* that!" I watched him try to figure when I had searched his room. It wasn't me, but my burglar friend who had found the hidden murder weapon.

Rupeka pulled the ice pick out of the floor. Its shaft was bent.

"A shocking accusation." I turned to Rupeka. "Could a crime lab detect any minute blood traces remaining on the pick?"

He nodded.

"Novak's motive for killing Lloyd Ames was simple," I said. "Hey, put that down."

Novak picked up his seltzer bottle and squeezed the handle twice, drenching Spillman. The clown sputtered and his greasepaint ran, making pastel tears.

My nostrils burned, and I knew it was gasoline, not water, in Novak's bottle. I remembered smelling something odd last night in Spillman's room. Shortly after, I had seen Novak puttering in the hall.

Rupeka closed in, halting midway when Novak pulled a butane lighter out of his pocket and waved it.

"Any closer, I torch Spillman," said Lorenz Novak, the exponent of Giggle Therapy.

I looked down at the book in my hand. It had a subtitle: *Health and Peace of Mind Through Laughter.* Sure. Novak's boffo one-liners were really bringing down the house today.

Time to begin my real performance.

I turned to Les Cook. "How many features has *Magazine Tonite* run on the Bermuda Triangle?"

"Huh?" Cook said, mesmerized by Novak's lighter. I repeated my question, and Cook shrugged.

"Your cameraman told me well over a dozen."

Novak, puzzled by my speech, didn't move his lighter any closer to Spillman.

I again faced the camera. "The media give wide, uncritical coverage to goofy notions like psychic surgery, UFOs on sightseeing tours of Earth, pyramid power, and mental key-bending. All myths, just like *Lorenz Novak.*"

"A man can't be a myth." Cook uttered his words slowly, as though talking to himself.

"I don't argue with all of Novak's ideas. In fact, after

using one of his tapes, I haven't smoked in fifteen hours. His *ideas* aren't mythical. Novak *himself* is."

"Shut up," Novak said, now sidling closer to Spillman.

"What's wrong? Lost your sense of humor, Lorenz? Want to hear a *real* joke? You, of all people, should appreciate this one. Did you hear the one about the man who healed his severe burns solely by mental power? It's a real knee-slapper. You've told this story so many times, and it's been printed so often, the public thinks it's true.

"But here are the facts. In 1960 the Burnette Boarding Home in Billings, Montana, burned to the ground—four people dead, eighteen injured. One of the survivors was a young man by the name of Bruce Hugo, a.k.a. Reverend Hugo Lawrence, a.k.a. Lorenz Novak. He suffered first-degree burns and was released from the hospital the next day. The cause of the fire was never determined, but officials suspected arson. The boardinghouse owner collected seventy-five thousand in insurance. What was your cut, Novak?"

Novak looked so damn jolly in his makeup, I couldn't gauge his reaction. Rupeka narrowed the distance to Novak by a step.

"At one time Lloyd Ames's sales territory for the Crown Laboratories Drug Company included Billings. He dealt with the same doctor that treated your burns, eventually learning you were lying about your past. He soon figured out a way to capitalize on it."

"Blackmail?" Jack said.

"Yep. In the beginning, Novak's payments satisfied Ames. They weren't exorbitant, so Novak considered them a mere irritation. But as the years passed, Novak's star began to shine, each book outselling the last. When Ames read the hype about the huge advance for Novak's next book, his demands skyrocketed far beyond Novak's means. Having become a victim of his own press, Novak was forced to eliminate Ames. You torched Ames's home, didn't you? Just as you torched that boardinghouse years

ago.'' I remembered Mrs. Ames saying how her family
had recently moved, *unexpectedly*.

"Ames escaped the fire with few burns," I said.

"So that's why he had ointment in his room," Jack said.

"Ames knew he had to kill Novak or be killed himself.
He stalked Novak around the country, ending up here at
the Fitch. Ames registered under the name of James Loy.
After the convention ended, he checked out but hid in a
vacant room. Sunday night he hired Kenneth Ratcliff, a
retired actor, to make him up like Quimp. The next morning, he was able to move around the hotel, knowing that
if he didn't talk, he wouldn't be noticed. While the others
were in the conference room, he ambushed Novak in the
hotel office, attacking him with a real ice pick. His down-
fall was in mistaking Novak for a *total* fraud, which he's
not. As we've all seen, Novak's in top physical shape."

Pride glimmered in Novak's face. Rupeka inched closer.

I went on. "Novak overpowered Ames, stabbed him with
his own ice pick, and stuffed the body in the safe, locking
it. He joined the other clowns in the conference room,
pretending nothing had happened. The body was discovered before he could find a gracious way to drop out of the
contest and leave town, but he was relieved to see that the
sheriff was using the murder of Ames to cover up his own
murder of Perry Vaughn. Later, I started asking questions,
scaring both Novak and the sheriff."

Novak said, "I'd love to hear the rest of your story, Mr.
Colderwood, but there's work to do. I'm saving the demolition crew lots of trouble. I've planted gasoline all over
the hotel. As we speak, on an upper floor there's a burning
candle with a fuse wrapped around it. The fuse leads out
into the hall, down the stairway, and into a room whose
rug is soaked with gasoline. That fuse should ignite any
minute now. Isn't that funny? Come on. *Laugh*. Are you
an audience or a funeral? Hey, I've got a million of them!
Let go. Laughing is good for you. You'll live longer.
Maybe *this* will make you laugh."

He flicked the wheel on his cigarette lighter, and its blue flame burned straight.

I waved my hands up and down, cuing everyone to laugh. Someone managed a metallic chuckle, then everyone joined in. Cook laughed the loudest. I noted that perspiration had conquered his hair spray, collapsing his coiffure.

Seeing his chance, Tarrant started for the lobby doors. Wirfel wheeled away from the sheriff and leveled his guns on Novak. Cate upended her miniature milk can, scattering hundreds of gumballs on the floor. Tarrant's hands paddled the air, and his feet did an impossible dance. He landed face down on gumballs. Dazed. Groaning.

"Nice work, Cate," Novak said. "Now if you'll kindly drop the guns, Deputy?"

Wirfel stuck to his guns.

Novak said, "I heard physical humor is in. Shall we see?" He spritzed his bottle lightly. A mist of gasoline drifted to the rug. Kneeling, he touched the lighter to it. A two-foot oval flame erupted, and Spillman shrank back. Rupeka stomped the rug, leaving a charred hole.

Novak laughed and said, "Wonderful timing, Mr. Rupeka—all-important in comedy. Drop them, Deputy. Now!"

Wirfel eased both guns to the floor, but Novak said, "No, throw them behind you. Hard."

The deputy reluctantly picked up the guns, and for a moment, I thought he was going to take his chances and open fire. He pitched one, then the other, bouncing them off the wall at the far end of the lobby.

"Your gun too, Mr. Rupeka. Don't look at me like I'm crazy. I know about the pistol strapped to your leg. No, not that clown gun. The real one. That's it. Take it out slowly. Good."

Rupeka whaled his gun across the lobby, and it hit the floor with a thump.

There was another thump. Closer. I turned and saw Jack

lying on his side, clutching his chest, his face tight with pain.

Rupeka rushed toward him. "Stay back," Novak said.

"He needs help," Rupeka said.

Novak grinned. "This is rich. The guy lives a tension-filled life and sucks on cigars all day. His heart's finally paying back the gratitude, and I'm supposed to pity him? He should have listened to me and learned to relax. Learned to laugh. If only he had—oh, go ahead. Help him. Let's let him live long enough to enjoy our little party."

Jack lost consciousness, and Rupeka motioned for Cate.

After Cate unbuttoned Jack's shirt, Rupeka pounded his chest and gave mouth-to-mouth.

"How are you going to get away with this, Novak?" I said.

"I'm not. When I turn the Fitch into a July Fourth celebration, *I'm* going to be one of the firecrackers, too." He soaked himself, and then Hodge, with gasoline. He also caught Spillman again with the spray. Whimpering, Hodge rubbed his hands over his costume, as if he could brush away the gasoline.

Novak said, "I figured all your snooping would lead to this. There's no cavalry to save you today."

So Novak was the one who abducted me. Having used a computer to write his books, he would know how to put that kidnap message on a floppy disk. His publisher had said Novak had zapped a whole book—accidentally erased it electronically. Fortunately for me, he had failed to zap his computerized kidnap message.

I looked at my watch. Could I stall for fifteen minutes?

"Aren't you violating your personal philosophy?" I asked.

"No. Quite the contrary. This will be my final experiment. Having already had minor surgery without anaesthetic, I now look forward to the challenge of the flames, to see if I can turn off that ultimate pain."

"Another Joan of Arc, right? Novak, you've anaesthetized yourself to more than just pain. You should have stuck to your phony healing act in those backwater towns.''

Novak lowered the bottle a few inches. "You've uncovered the rest?"

"You shouldn't have worried. Those pictures of the evangelical groups and faith healers in the hotel basement wouldn't have blown your cover. They were too faded for anyone to recognize you. Ames's excessive blackmailing panicked you. One reason you came back to the Fitch was to see if any link to your past still existed, right? The Fitch was once a popular stopover for the circuit you were on. It was during those faith-healing days that you learned some basic sleight of hand, enough to help Spillman with his practice. Amazing how a little parlor magic can jazz up a bogus healing demonstration. You were tired of hiring stooges to fake rejuvenation. Your game of pretending to extract tumors, using palmed chicken parts, was growing wearisome, too. You wanted respectability, so you underwent a metamorphosis from Reverend Hugo Lawrence to Lorenz Novak, the man who heals with jokes. But look at you now: standing there in a clown suit, showing the world that *you* are the biggest joke of all.''

"You can't—"

"Freeze, Novak. Put the lighter down. Then the bottle," Rupeka said. He held a pistol in a two-handed grip.

Novak's red-rimmed clown eyes widened. "Another gun?" His lips moved slowly as he tried to calculate how he had missed this weapon. His face lit up, as bright as the clown face on Spillman's electric button. "Oh, shit. That's the gun you and Cate used in the bullet-catching. Forget it, Rupeka. It's fake. It doesn't shoot real bullets. I know. Colderwood told me himself.''

Struggling to ignore him, Rupeka said, "Easy now. Drop the lighter. I can pump one slug into you, maybe two, before you light it." Keeping his head still, Rupeka flicked his eyes at me. I wondered how much he knew about stage magic. Did he really know whether the gun was fake?

I thought of how Rupeka shooting his wife's lover re-
sulted in unbearable pressure for him.

"Go ahead. Pull the trigger. It won't stop me. I'm hot
tonight. Great audience. Just starting to cook," Novak said.

He ignited the lighter and started for Spillman. Rupeka
tightened his grip on the gun, and it quivered up and down
like a small animal trying to escape.

Novak waved the flame at Spillman, who stared passively at his would-be executioner.

Novak said, "Fire away, officer. I mean, ex-officer. That
might as well be a cap pistol. It's as phony as Colderwood
the Magician. As fake as—"

"As fake as Lorenz Novak?" I said.

But no one heard.

Rupeka pulled the trigger, and the blast ripped into Novak's shoulder, spinning him. Novak went down, still
holding on to his lighter. Its flame snapped out. Spillman
reared back his size-eighteen shoe and punted the lighter
out of Novak's hand.

Rupeka's expression was all grimace and teeth. The gun
looked welded to his hands.

Novak struggled to sit up. He touched his hand to his
shoulder, and it came away red. Concentrating on his
shoulder, he closed his eyes tight and opened them, as if
expecting to heal the wound mentally. Novak seemed in
no pain, his face serene.

Hodge grabbed Novak's ragged coat lapels. "Which
room? Which room's that candle in?"

When Novak told him, Hodge stripped off his gasoline-
soaked costume down to his underwear and ran for the
stairway.

I became aware again of Ray's camera and the whirring
tape machine.

"Enough, Ray. Shut her off."

Les Cook insisted that Ray move in for close-ups of
Novak. Apparently the meter had run out on the money I
had slipped the cameraman. He obeyed Cook, walking past
the trembling, frozen Rupeka, and moving to within a foot

of the bleeding Novak. He captured an ultra-close shot of Novak's blood-soaked coat.

"Turn it off," I said.

He ignored me, getting a shot of the expression on Novak's face. I went over to Ray and jerked the camera out of his hands. I pulled the cassette out of his recorder and smashed it. I ripped and stretched and tore as much tape as I could.

I went to call an ambulance, but Jack was already at the switchboard. He winked at me, and I realized he had faked the heart attack so he could pass the gun to Rupeka.

What a phony.

What a roomful of goddam phonies.

"The case against me is weak," Tarrant said. His hands were cuffed behind him, but he conducted himself with authority. "The evidence is hearsay and circumstantial. Also, tearing up that videotape was stupid. Not that I'm complaining."

"I don't expect you to understand why I destroyed the tape," I said, "but I do agree that a murder rap against you will have problems. It will also be tough to prove that the coroner and the undertaker were under your thumb. That's why I decided on something simpler."

We watched two medical attendants lower a stoic Novak onto a stretcher. As they wheeled Novak toward us, he asked them to stop. They told him to make it fast.

Novak, oblivious of his shoulder wound, looked at me with wonder and said, "I thought you told me that bullet-catching is all trickery."

"It is, but I never said the *gun* was fake."

"If the gun's real, how did you catch the bullet?"

"That's a secret. Magicians never expose secrets."

"Bullshit. If you weren't so bent on exposing everyone's secrets, none of this would have happened. Get me the hell out of here," he said to the white suits, and they trundled him away.

On the way out the front door, they passed Duane Jeffers

as he entered the hotel lobby. I looked at my watch. Twenty minutes late. I introduced Tarrant to Jeffers. When I stated the latter's occupation, Tarrant's haughtiness caved in.

"Jeffers has an amazing record. Duane, how many of your tax-evasion cases in the past six years have been found not guilty?"

Jeffers made a zero sign with his forefinger and his thumb. I walked over to the sheet-covered chair and picked up the padded envelope of books that the burglar had "borrowed" from Tarrant's office and home.

"You're a meticulous person, Tarrant. I bet you even know how many paper clips are in your desk. I was hoping you were compulsive enough to keep *these* kind of records, too." I opened the first ledger and turned to a page headed VAUGHN. "This section alone lists all the cuts you took from Vaughn's protection operation. There are other cash gifts entered here, for other services you've provided. I understand you have quite a reputation in town for doing favors. I'm glad to see you kept close records of them."

I handed the book to Jeffers. After studying one page, he closed it and gave it back to me.

"Aren't you going to read the rest?" I said.

"Later. That page alone is worth five years. How many pages are there? Fifty?" He made a mental calculation and whistled. "I hated cutting my vacation short, but for something like this . . ." He smiled. It was the smile of man about to feast after a grueling day's labor.

Tarrant bristled. "That's theft. You can't use those books as evidence."

I took the book back from Jeffers and picked up the others. "No. It's not theft. It's *illusion.*" I tossed all the books into the air. As soon as they left my fingertips, they turned into a handful of metallic confetti and fluttered to the floor. "The *real* books are probably hidden in your home . . . in a place you can't remember. That's too bad. If you could remember where they are, you could tell a friend to pick them up before the IRS gets a search warrant for them. Things will get especially interesting if they can document through bank records any big purchases you've made and also if you've lived far beyond your stated means.''

Tarrant's face went death gray. I stuffed something under his arm.

"Here. You'll need this. It helped me. Especially the first part on adopting a healthy, positive outlook on life."

It was Novak's book.

watch. I started with the fuse, the same one Novak had

EPILOGUE

Six months later.

One-fifty A.M.

Parked across the street from a convenience store called Mom and Pop's—the former site of the Fitch Hotel.

Concrete monoliths, the beginnings of a parking garage, stood where the Edison Building had been.

My van's engine wanted to quit. I nursed it by tapping the gas. It needed a mechanic. Maybe tomorrow.

Two boxes sat on the front seat. I put one under my arm and climbed out. I left the motor running, not wanting to stay in Roselle a minute longer than necessary.

The front of the store was lit up like a barroom jukebox, a far cry from Kaufman's Confectionery of my childhood. Though the air was still, the cold bit my fingers. They'd be numb by the time I finished. I picked a spot in the parking lot midway between the self-serve gas pumps and the store, close to where the hotel entrance used to be.

A scrawny man, made fat by layered clothing, sat on a bus-stop bench by the store entrance. I could see the dingy white of his socks through the rips in his shoes.

Inside, a Mom and Pop's clerk, wearing a smock and hat with pictures of hot dogs on them, sloshed his mop back and forth. The plastic banner above the entrance said, "Grand Opening." I was going to make it grander.

I opened my box and spread my materiel out onto the parking-lot blacktop. The man on the bench wandered over to watch. I started with the fuse, the same one Novak had tried to booby-trap the Fitch with.

The man told me his name was Jonesy and asked if I needed a hand with anything. I gave him an end to hold while I uncoiled the fuse.

Mop in hand, the clerk stood in the doorway and yelled, "Jesus Christ! What do you think you're doing? Get out!"

Preoccupied with my mini-arsenal, I didn't hear what else he said.

I laid out the flash paper and smoke powder. A few pieces of flash paper, a standard magician's prop, cost several dollars. I had purchased eight pounds, in nine different colors—two hundred dollars' worth. One thin piece the size of a napkin was enough to make a fireball twice the size of a basketball. I had smoke powder, too, in four colors.

When the storekeeper didn't leave, I stood up straight and gave him a killer stare. For a moment he weighed his life against the minimum wage, then retreated inside, deciding it was safer to threaten me through the intercom attached to the gas pumps.

What the intercom speaker took away in clarity, it added in menace. The clerk sounded mean as he threatened to call the cops.

A sedan with a red star on its door pulled in behind my van. "Cops are already here," I said, but the clerk couldn't hear me. I hadn't pushed TALK on the intercom.

The old man said, "You one of them political radicals? Or did you kidnap somebody? Why do you want to blow up the goddam store?" He adjusted his camouflage hat. "Am I going to be on TV?"

He asked again what I was doing, and why. I tried explaining, but all I did was ramble, thoroughly confusing Jonesy. I even told him about Cate. When I finished, he humored me by feigning interest.

"Now let me get this straight. You really fell for this woman, but you just let her go?" he said.

"That's true. I haven't heard from Cate Fleming since that last day at the Fitch. Rupeka lied to me. Cate's husband knew what was going on between us. Before he had his change of heart, Rupeka sent Phil Fleming those secretly made recordings of her and me, along with my phone conversations. On that last afternoon at the Fitch, a black car arrived, and a chauffeur carried out all Cate's baggage from the hotel, including her portable exercise bike.''

Jonesy whistled and shook his head.

"Before she left, I saw her sitting in the limo, wearing headphones, listening to the tapes her husband sent with the chauffeur. She came back into the hotel and said these three words to me: 'How could you?' She called her husband and told him she didn't know if she'd be coming home. Next she called her agent and fired him. Then she called a cab and waited for it. Outside.

"She had left a tape recorder on the lobby desk. I turned it on and heard myself talking to Cate's agent, posing as a film producer. Of course the reason I made those calls was to see if Salny was under Phil Fleming's thumb, but she wouldn't listen to my explanation. She told me I was no less a manipulator than her husband, and then she said she wanted to be alone to sort out whether she and I had any future together. That's the last I've seen or heard of Cate. I called her husband a few months back, but he doesn't know where she's living, either. You know, Jonesy, I keep watching those aspirin ads on TV, but they're using a new actress now.''

"This Cate, is she a radical, too?''

Ignoring his question, I dumped out a jar of flash powder and leveled the pile of white with my foot.

"What was that you tried to tell me about a guy that collected clowns?'' Jonesy said.

"I was just saying that nobody will ever see the character of Quimp portrayed again. The costume and all the props are now gathering dust in the collection of Gregory Hodge. Who knows in what part of the world Hodge is now, haggling over another conquest for his holdings? The character of Quimp will remain his least expensive and hardest-won acquisition.''

I took Jonesy's end of the fuse and wrapped it around the stack of the flash paper, tying it in tight overhand knots. I picked up the reel of fuse and walked backward toward my van, dropping a line of fuse as I went.

"Here, let me do that," he said, grabbing the reel from me and continuing to unwind the fuse. I walked backward with him.

"I never did get a chance to see if I liked trade shows. The news of the *Magazine Tonite* incident traveled ahead of me to Allentown. The production company refused to broadcast that segment of me at the Roselle post office. By the time I arrived, Stanley Trimble was already breaking in another magician. I asked for the five thousand that Jack O'Connell sent him. Trimble denied receiving it, but I persuaded him to give it to me."

"How?"

"I offered to teach him a famous magical feat: the amazing Bullet-Catching Feat."

Jonesy laughed. It was the kind of laugh reserved for close friends, for equals. Did he consider me a brother? He scratched his growth of beard, and I found myself scratching my face, too. Its rasp was just as loud as his. In a beard-growing contest I would have won.

"Trimble gave me the whole five thousand. I paid nearly all of it to a private detective to track down Michelle Blue and warn her that former Sheriff Virgil Tarrant was out on bond, that her life could be in danger. Tarrant was furious that she skipped out on him, and I knew he was capable of killing again. He was the one that put the bullet hole in Novak's windshield. Tarrant figured out that Novak was the one that kidnapped me, and he was angry that Novak couldn't let things alone. That's good, Jonesy, there's plenty of fuse. Just let it roll out."

Jonesy looked both ways before we stepped off the sidewalk and walked backward across the street.

"I hired a pro because I didn't want to waste time and money tracking down Michelle, Jonesy. If you want a job done right, always hire a pro. Speaking of Sheriff Tarrant, last I heard, his trial on tax evasion is up soon. Right?''

''Don't read the papers. Sorry.''

Making sure my back was to the fuse, I lit up a cigarette and savored the taste. The effects of my session with Novak's tape had worn off, and I was smoking more than ever. I guess you have to have faith in whatever system you use. Novak wasn't much of an inspiration. *Pseudophysician, heal thyself.*

The van's engine sputtered and died. A car door slammed, and we both turned around. The hood went up on my van, and I saw someone taking a peek at the innards. Jonesy and I continued our back-stepping journey across the street.

''For a while they were afraid that Rupeka wasn't going to recover from shooting Novak, but he's making progress now, thanks to Spillman. While at the Fitch, Spillman realized he could only learn so much about magic on his own. He needed someone to spend endless hours coaching him. Spillman bought a hunting camp and ten thousand dollars' worth of video cameras and recorders, and he and Rupeka are holed up there right now. Practicing. The last postcard I received from Spillman said that they were averaging twelve hours a day. I wouldn't be surprised if five years from now I walked into a Vegas lounge and saw Marcus Spillman, with Rupeka as his manager, wowing them with his close-up magic.

''The same day I got Spillman's card, I received notification of Jack O'Connell's death. You know who I mean, Jonesy? He used to own the hotel that was on this lot.''

He shook his head. ''I just hit town a few weeks ago. This used to be a hotel?''

''Jack's fake heart attack was either prophetic or not entirely fake. The executor of his estate informed me that Jack had an unusual last request. That's what I'm doing here tonight. This is my tribute to Jack.''

''Did this Jack leave you anything other than his memory?''

"No. No money. He knew me too well to try that."

We reached the van where Sam Wirfel, the town's new sheriff, had just completed hooking jumper cables to my van.

I reached in my pocket and took out a cigarette lighter and a roll of bills—all the money left after paying the private detective. I put the cash in Jonesy's pocket and handed him the lighter. He frowned. Apparently, others had given him sizable handouts before, and he was waiting for the catch.

"Hey, buddy, you don't intend to . . . uh . . . do anything funny do you?"

"No, don't worry. Let me tell you about that lighter you're holding. It used to belong to a famous writer who advocated laughter, but lost his own sense of humor. He just made publishing history. His new book on health just set the record for the most books printed but never distributed. That's a lot of warehouse space. At least my TV special doesn't take up much space in its little canister. Did I tell you there's a defense fund for Novak? Yeah, a cult of his believers are making sure that he gets the best lawyers for his trial. When I give you the signal, just light the fuse. Enjoy yourself, Jonesy."

He saluted me.

Wirfel walked around from the front of the van and opened up the door of his squad car. He said, "When I give her gas, try starting it."

I climbed in the van and looked at the box beside me. I had been thinking more and more of that day the clowns did their outside show, of how the demolition workers tossed spare change and bills in appreciation. Now *that* would a nice way to earn a living. No company, no badmouthing agents, no government, and no assistants. Just me, a few pieces of magic equipment, a street corner, and something for—

"For Christ's sake, start it. I don't have all night," Wirfel said.

The starter moaned and caught right up. Wirfel got out,

unhooked the cables, and coiled them. Stopping outside my window, he said, "You ought to invest in a set of these."

"You been following me?"

"Since you hit town, and I'll dog you until you leave. Just pray your heap doesn't break down before you make it out."

"You'd better hop in your squad car. I'm leaving now."

Wirfel pretended not to see Jonesy holding the fuse in one hand and the lighter in the other.

"Just don't ever come back to Roselle," Wirfel said, getting in his car.

I pulled away and gave Jonesy the thumbs-up sign. He lit the fuse.

After I drove two blocks, Jack's memorial, like silent fireworks, lit the sky behind me.

I lifted the lid on the box beside me. Inside was a top hat that I would never wear. Nor would I use it in a trick.

At the Roselle city limits, I pulled over and checked my road map for the nearest city. I'd get there early to pick the best street corner. I hoped it would be a profitable one— one where passersby who liked my magic would drop me spare change.

In my brand-new top hat.